T0094604

HERE AND SOMEWHERE ELSE

HERE AND SOMEWHERE ELSE

—

GRACE PALEY AND
ROBERT NICHOLS

WITH AN INTRODUCTION BY
MARIANNE HIRSCH

The Feminist Press
at The City University of New York
New York

Published in 2007 by the Feminist Press at the City University of New York, The Graduate Center, 365 Fifth Avenue, Suite 5406, New York, NY 10016

Library of Congress Cataloging-in-Publication Data
Paley, Grace.
  Here and somewhere else / Grace Paley and Robert Nichols ; with an introduction by Marianne Hirsch.
    p. cm. -- (2 x 2 series)
  ISBN-13: 978-1-55861-537-3 (pbk.)
  ISBN-10: 1-55861-537-7 (pbk.)
  I. Nichols, Robert, 1919- II. Title.
  PS3566.A46H47 2007
  811'.54--dc22

                              2006026135

Text and cover design by Lisa Force
Printed in Canada

13 12 11 10 09 08 07   5 4 3 2 1

CONTENTS

—

INTRODUCTION

—

"You don't have a story," Grace Paley recently told me, "until you have two stories. At least two stories. That's what I always tell my students." Two stories. Two writers. Grace Paley and Robert Nichols. Two by two. This volume tells (at least) two stories of two writers: one, a woman, daughter of Russian Jewish immigrants, a poet, short story writer, essayist, feminist, political activist; the other, a man, son of Canadian and New England Protestants, a landscape architect, theater director, poet, novelist, short story writer, activist. And, in telling two stories, it tells one, braided by their life together, by the conversations and arguments they share as a writing couple living on a hilltop in Vermont, active participants in the political life of the second half of the twentieth century and now also the twenty first. Their political commitments and ethical values, their desire to heal the world, could not be more similar; their themes and writing styles, the ways in which they think and talk about their writing, could not be more different. And yet, reading them both, creating one story out of two, brings us back to Grace Paley's comment: two stories are a conversation; they expose the core of storytelling in the acts of telling and listening. Two stories are multiple stories, infinite in their interrelations.

In preparing to introduce this volume, I visited Paley

and Nichols in their Thetford Hill home in Vermont. It was a sultry summer day and even on their hilltop, overlooking the contours of Smarts Mountain, the humidity was high and no breeze was blowing. We had set aside an hour to talk about the stories and poems in this volume and about their work. Driving up the steep hill, the visitor is invariably struck by the natural beauty of the hillside, the rich and unruly flower and vegetable gardens and the myriad toys lying around the yard, always ready for the four young grandchildren (two of his and two of hers) who visit daily. When I arrived, Nichols was emerging from the woods where, as he often does, he was working, clearing brush. Paley was sitting on a chair surrounded by two visitors from Hanoi, Minh Ha and Thanh Binh, who had come to stay for a few days. As we sat down to work, the visitors listened to our conversation and told us about their plans to translate some of Paley's work into Vietnamese. Meanwhile, Paley went to find photos of her recent visit to Hanoi, while Nichols questioned the visitors about current economic conditions in Vietnam. Vermont tends to be busy in the summer, with tourists and visitors stopping by for a few hours or a few days, but there is no busier place than the Paley/Nichols home. During my visit, the phone rang repeatedly, and the Fedex truck drove up and Nichols went to chat with the driver. Soon the writer Gish Jen stopped by on her way to New York to give Paley a hug: she stayed a while to chat with the Hanoi feminists. Many stories in the space of an hour—a typical hour leading up to a lunch of a delicious vegetable soup (made from their own squash, peppers and potatoes), bread and cheese, all served on a kitchen table cluttered with mail, magazines, books, and flyers about local, national, and international events and calls to action. The remote Vermont hilltop is as busy and as engaging as the New York street corners on which Paley often sets her stories. The open house, the lively discussions about local and global issues, the books and phone calls, and even the interruptions shape the writing as much as the life. Here and everywhere.

When asked how he would contextualize his work, Robert Nichols answers unequivocally: "I come from the sixties." For him the sixties are the antiwar movement, on the one hand, and the aesthetic avant-garde on the other. It was the moment one could do absolutely anything with form, he says somewhat wistfully. It's a freedom he has stubbornly held on to.

Robert Nichols was born in Worcester, Massachusetts in 1919, but spent his adolescent summers in Vermont. After boarding school, college, and service in the Pacific during the Second World War, he studied with Walter Gropius at the Harvard Graduate School of Design. He chose landscape architecture as a means to focus on the outdoors and the community, but, after graduation, his employers asked him to design highways and shopping malls. Nichols married Mary Perot, a columnist for the *Village Voice*, and had two daughters and a son.

It was Nichols's work in New York in the sixties that opened up possibilities of community involvement in building parks and playgrounds and in restoring buildings on the Lower East Side to create safe havens for young rebels and runaways. He was one of the community architects who redesigned Washington Square Park, winning a fight against Robert Moses's ambition to divide the park to expand Fifth Avenue. The three mounds he added to the park—mounds used by generations of children and adults to hone their climbing and sledding skills, and by performers to create a natural amphitheater—are now, once again, threatened with demolition. His design work and his political commitments led him to the theater—he founded the Judson Poets' Theater, wrote plays that were performed there and at the Public Theater, and staged numerous street theater performances in protest against the Vietnam war.

Nichols had always written poetry and staged plays, and he had always studied history, economics, and Marxism. His turn to fiction was motivated by his political ideas and he chose to write a utopian novel for what he considered its social "usefulness" to readers who might want to reenvision their living conditions. His tetralogy *Daily Lives in Nghsi-Altai* (1977, 1979) follows four Westerners who visit an eponymous country, whose political and social structures are the opposite of the United States. His "comic fiction" *From the Steam Room* (1993) paints a surreal New York City on the verge of collapse and the efforts to salvage it by corrupt and all-too-familiar historical characters from the world of politics and high finance. Nichols has published several volumes of poetry, *Slow Newsreel of Man Riding Train* (1962),

Address to the Smaller Animals (1976), and *Red Shift* (1977), as well as *In the Air* (1991), a volume of short fiction. His most recent comic novel *Simple Gift* follows the member of a back-to-the-land commune to the multinational corporation for which he works in Calcutta, eventually bringing his entire commune with him after they attend a Green film festival there. Here, as in his earlier work, Nichols faces the challenges of political fiction: how to incorporate historical events and archival documents, such as newspaper articles, into an invented fictional world. Nichols's novels are also punctuated by poetry (the two financiers in *From the Steam Room* seek solace in the poems they exchange), just as his poems often have a narrative structure.

It is this formal freedom, this bold mixture of genres—poetry and prose, fiction and essay—that characterizes Nichols' writing, as well as the deliberate inattention to plot and to character development or psychological depth. His transgressions of generic distinctions and of the conventions of realist narrative spawn a literature of ideas in the tradition of the eighteenth-century French philosophers Diderot and Voltaire (his chosen predecessors), and, I would add, the twentieth-century German playwright and theorist of political theater Bertolt Brecht. From Franz Kafka he takes a profound sensitivity to contradiction and incommensurability. And from the theater he gets the sense of montage, of experiment, of scenarios, and the rehearsal of repetitions and alternate versions rather than plot or linearity.

Although she is only three years younger than Nichols, Grace Paley narrates her writing origins in quite different terms. If he "come(s) from the sixties," she sees herself as emerging from the 1950s and from the company of women living and working within or, rather, in proximity to a strongly masculine intellectual scene. She remembers being fully aware of the profound rift between men and women—the men who had returned from the war and the women who had passed the days and evenings caring for the kids and talking to each other. Married to cameraman Jess Paley, she spent her days in the park with her daughter and her son and made women friends for life. And she wrote poems and stories. For her, the sixties were the women's movement and the conversations it generated among women, who fueled her early stories. "When I came to think as a writer, it was because I had begun to live among women," she writes (*Just as I Thought*, 168). No doubt, living among women in the fifties and trying to write and get published would not have presented itself as an endless horizon. There were a number of casualties of that era—Sylvia Plath and Anne Sexton come easily to mind—and only someone of Paley's courage and optimism would see, from the start, the rich possibilities contained in the identity of the "housewife" who wants to be a writer. This is, in fact, how she was described in her early reviews.

Paley was born in the Bronx in 1922; her parents were recent immigrants from Ukraine and she was surrounded by Yiddish, Russian, and the many dialects of English of

New York's boroughs. The Bronx streets in which she grew up and the landscapes of Greenwich Village where she lived most of her adult life, form the settings of stories peopled by the women and men of her generation and surroundings, engaged in the dailiness of their lives. Her writing is driven by the languages and voices around her. Paley studied at Hunter College and then New York University, briefly; she studied with W.H. Auden at the New School for Social Research, but never completed a degree. She taught creative writing at Sarah Lawrence College for twenty-two years, taught as a visiting writer at Columbia, Syracuse, City College, and Dartmouth, and she regularly teaches creative-writing workshops at the Fine Arts Work Center in Provincetown. "The assignments I give are usually assignments I've given myself, problems that have defeated me, investigations I'm still pursuing," she writes about her teaching (*Just as I Thought*, 191).

Paley, who had primarily written poems during her childhood and youth, published her first short story collection *The Little Disturbances of Man* in 1959. It was followed by *Enormous Changes at the Last Minute: Stories* (1974), *Later the Same Day* (1985), and *The Collected Stories* (1994). The short fiction stands alongside her volumes of poetry *Leaning Forward* (1985) and *Begin Again: Collected Poems* (2000); her book of essays and speeches *Just as I Thought* (1998); and her volume of poetry and prose *Long Walks and Intimate Talks* (1991).

Like Nichols's, Paley's writing career should be seen in relation to the other story—her political activism in the civil rights and the women's movements, and in the struggle for

7

peace and justice in many different areas. Since the 1950s, she has worked with, supported, and founded a number of groups, including the War Resisters League, the Women's Pentagon Action, The Clamshell Alliance, Resist, the Feminist Press, and Madre, to name only a few. She is active in PEN, particularly in the struggles against censorship and as a founder of the PEN Women's Committee (According to *Women's World*, this committee was established in 1986 because at the 48th Congress of PEN only 16 of 117 speakers were women and Pres. Norman Mailer "said this was because 1) the writers had to be of 'real distinction'; 2) other women had been invited but didn't come; and 3) this was an intellectual setting and the only woman intellectual was Susan Sontag" [1994]). Paley traveled to Hanoi on a 1969 Peace Mission and to Moscow as a delegate to the 1974 World Peace Conference. In 1979, she organized the first feminist environmental conference, "Women and Life on Earth."

Paley and Nichols met at the Greenwich Village Peace Center, at what they call "a very small action" in 1960–61—the organized resistance against the construction of nuclear shelters, which they were eager to reveal as government scare tactics. They married in 1972, spent their honeymoon in Chile, and live in New York and Vermont, where Nichols continues to be active in Rural Vermont, an organization dedicated to saving small farms. Paley was named the first official writer of New York State and, more recently, Vermont's Poet Laureate. Together, Paley and Nichols taught as Montgomery Fellows at Dartmouth College, and they frequently give readings together. The publishing house they established together, Glad Day Books, was dedicated to publishing political writing that might otherwise have difficulty finding a publisher. Well into their eighties, they continue to argue the world, working in local and global politics together, mostly with their Thetford affinity group, and never missing a peace vigil or demonstration.

During our conversation on Thetford Hill, both Paley and Nichols insisted on the differences that marked their writing. He writes in response to a political problem or an idea about the world, while she writes "because I heard someone say something." She has described herself as a "story hearer." They claim to have the same literary tastes, even though they argue about many other things. They share the experience of reading out loud to each other, every night. They read long novels, most recently Amos Oz's *Fima*, and they plan to read *Middlemarch* soon. And, Paley exclaimed, "We share the Bread and Puppet Theater!" Indeed both have supported, performed with, written for and about Bread and Puppet, and marched with them at demonstrations for the last thirty years. The aesthetics and politics of Bread and Puppet provide an illuminating introduction to Paley's and Nichols' stories and poems. The enormous puppets made of fabric and paper; the larger than life colorless villains (capitalists, war mongers, the military industrial complex, always in gray suits); the suffering victims (the washerwomen, wearing

9

kerchiefs); and the luminous saviors (Mother Earth, Nature): All tell a simple ur-story that Paley and Nichols play with and complicate in their own writing.

On the Vermont hillsides where the pageants are staged, audiences participate and follow the puppets, eating bread and garlic prepared by the performers. There, just as in Paley's and Nichols's stories, political plots are hatched, astute analyses of political forces emerge in simple, often comical form, and anger is transformed into humor and action. In her tribute to Bread and Puppet in *Just as I Thought*, Paley reiterates one line, a line which could apply to herself and to Nichols as well: "Why not speak the truth directly? Just speak out! Speak to! Why not?" Two questions and two exclamations. Both writers certainly speak out in whatever they write. Paley, perhaps more than Nichols, speaks to, addresses, and engages her reader directly. And both have that sense of experimentation and questioning suggested by the "Why Not?" Each insists that the other is the most truthful person he/she knows.

Both Paley's and Nichols's writing confounds conventional generic distinctions. Sidra DeKoven Ezrahi has written that Paley is a scribe of urban prose and a poet of the country (Ezrahi 2006, 1200). Nichols's poetry could be described as more domestic, his prose as more global. But both also defy attempts at classification. Both feel that writing poetry makes the writer more attentive to language and form in the writing of prose, while writing prose gives the poetry more freedom.

In "How to Tell a Story (My Method) (Most of the Time)," Paley asserts the profound interconnections between poetry and prose: "Find the paragraph to/hold the poem steady/for six to eight pages . . . don't let her lose the poem/in the telling of day by/day" (*Begin Again*, 142). Paley and Nichols both mix autobiography and fiction and, although each revels in precise detail, those details veer off into the absurd, the grotesque, or the surreal: neither writes in the inherited conventions of realism. In Nichols's "Reading the Meter," for example, the protagonist Goss receives his electricity bill: "Besides the usual sheet of paper giving the bill period—June 15th to July 15th and the rate—there was an additional item. Eight people killed in the village of Jinoteca, Nicaragua. Externalities $31.00." Everything follows from this startling incongruous, and utterly implausible plot detail: Goss's obsessive effort to speak to the meter reader, his phone calls to the electric company, the "testimonio" of a dying Nicaraguan from Jinoteca, the detailed description of the meter itself. Fact turned to fiction, fiction capacious enough to incorporate political analysis, paranoia, exacting description.

Paley's "The Long-Distance Runner" also veers into the realm of fantasy, and also within the most seemingly realistic narrative and description. After training as a long-distance runner, Faith takes off one day to return to her old neighborhood in Brighton Beach. She is quickly "surrounded by at least three hundred blacks." The charged and slightly threatening conversations that ensue are fully plausible until Faith "jump(s) right in with some facts. I said, How many flowers' names do you know? Wildflowers, I mean." And the group begins supplying names of wildflowers. Details, speech patterns, descriptions, all paint the most realistic of pictures, but do not quite add up to a realistic tale. Threatened and afraid of the neighborhood youth, Faith eventually flees to her parents' former apartment and stays with Mrs. Luddy, her boy Donald, and three baby girls for three weeks, before taking off one morning, when Mrs Luddy tells her it is time to go home.

How are we to read the implausibilities in Paley's stories and in Nichols's? We might see them as allegories of the authors' political explorations: U.S. involvement in Central America, or the black/white relations in the midst of urban shifts in the New York boroughs. Or we might see them in the realm of the fantastic, the surreal, or superreal. But why try to confine these writers to forms or conventions they consistently challenge? I would suggest that each comes from a somewhat different impulse. "Reading the Meter" illustrates, in a comic, almost grotesque mode, the implication of every U.S. citizen in the untoward activities of government and big business abroad. Nichols is less interested in the protagonist Goss, or his wife, or the meter reader: they serve as vehicles to explore how mega-politics might work on a micro level if they were acknowledged. "What if?" the story's narrator seems to be asking. In "The Long-Distance Runner," on the other hand, the characters themselves, painted with only a few strokes, manage to gain some psychological depth and elicit our keen interest. Faith and Mrs.

Luddy interact over the space of a few pages. Their meeting is, in a sense, a failure: they do not become friends. Faith cannot go home again; her neighborhood, her apartment, is theirs now, no longer hers. And yet, the two women respect each other and each other's lives. These are the ideas of the story. But Paley also conveys Faith's restlessness, her dissatisfaction with her own life, her fear and curiosity about blacks, her affection for the boy Donald, her frustrated fantasies of reconnection with her old home. Here, on the level of character, voice and tone, the story gains an emotional impact and a different form of truth.

Alternatively, we might read "Reading the Meter" alongside Paley's poem "Here," a poem that, like Nichols's story, mentions the meter reader's visit in Vermont, but now as part of a touching love poem steeped in the dailiness of old age. No implausibilities here, just the speaker, "an old woman with heavy breasts," asserting happily and somewhat bemused by her own older self, "here I am." While she is "suddenly exhausted by my desire/ to kiss his sweet explaining lips," her "old man across the yard" is "talking to the meter reader. . . . telling him the world's sad story. . . ." This division of labor recalls, and transposes to a domestic setting, Paley's poem "Is There a Difference Between Men and Women," a series of declarative lines that distinguish, clearly, between those responsible for the arms trade, the slave trade, the trade in the bodies of women, and those engaged in the household trade, in the trade in the markets selling "melon mustard greens/ cloth shining dipped in/onion dye, beet grass."

Do Paley's and Nichols's stories and poems really support this traditional gender divide, do they illustrate differentially gendered sensibilities? Readers will have to make up their own minds, but they will have to be wary of any simple or straightforward answers. Certainly Nichols is first motivated by ideas, Paley by the observation of human behavior. She is passionately interested in women's and children's lives, in people's voices and in small stories. "It's hard to dislike people once you know them," Paley has written and there are, in fact, few villains in even her most political of stories. The racist white man in "Traveling" is one atypical villain who elicits hate, but even the threatening black boys in Brighton Beach in "The Long-Distance Runner" provoke our interest and our sympathy. Nichols claims that his primary subject is economic policy and his villains, like the giant white-faced and bloody-handed capitalist Bread and Puppet characters, are the three men from the World Bank in "Peasants," or the oblivious cinema goers in "The Mirror of Narcissus." Neither villains nor heroes gain much depth, however. Is this differential approach to character gendered—is it even consistent? Nichols's poems could perhaps be seen to belie that: the father-son relationship in "Father and Son on the Road," for example, emerges fully drawn in that poem.

Both Paley and Nichols teach us how to read their work. "The Mirror of Narcissus" may be Robert Nichols's most explicit poetic manifesto. Like many of Nichols's and Paley's fictions, it breaks down into two stories, and it also thematizes the desire for the second story, the anxiety about being able to tell it. The writer, Hawthorne, is caught in his own world, staring into the pool, like Narcissus, unable to break out of the enchanting self-reflection that soon becomes boring. Out of the pool, another face stares up at him—a listener? A reader? An unreachable Other? But "the writer, Hawthorne, confronts a double barrier." He dislikes writing about the very people who are his readers, and he is unable, through the medium of fiction, to account for "large numbers," for the people of the foreign country, Italy, that he is visiting. His gaze is too diffuse, his knowledge too thin. The people of Italy for Hawthone in the 1800s are the people of the barrio of Los Gatos for Nichols. He imagines them in different situations, illustrating the economic concept of "underemployment." "Can the mirror be broken?" Can the writer, who is here, write about somewhere else? Nichols tries, in this story, as in "Peasants." He tries to account for large numbers, writes from a distance, places his characters, as a theater director would, into various scenarios, examining various economic conditions. But he remains unsure of his right to speak, definitively, about that somewhere else.

One telling meta-fictional detail illuminates Nichols's fiction: the binoculars in "Reading the Meter." When Goss looks through the binoculars his family gave him for his birthday, he begins to get closer to things, the birds that were only identifiable by their sound, the meter reader who was previously elusive, Miss Johnson of the Electric Company who is personalized in his daughter's account of the concert where she met her and saw her cry. Perhaps his wife and daughter gave him the binoculars so that he might look at them, rather than having, always, his head somewhere else. In his fiction, Nichols often chooses to put the binoculars away and to examine larger forces from a distance. At other times, he looks through them and focuses closely, ruthlessly, on human, and political, contradictions and inequities.

Paley's writing is on a different scale, always in extremely close focus, though the details she brings into view often have far-ranging symbolic import. One need only think of the maple that fights to live in "Walking in the Woods," or the child's voice that urges the speaker to "begin again," in the poem by that title, or the marks on the skin in "Three Days and a Question." Mostly, however, the conversations in Paley's fictional and autobiographical stories capture us for their very own concentrated interest. And for what they can tell us about stories and their telling. In "Debts," Paley raises the question of what the writer owes to the stories of others, a question not unrelated to that of Nichols in "The Mirror of Narcissus." She concludes that "I did owe something to my own family and the families of my friends. That is to tell their stories as simply as possible in order, you might say, to save a few lives." Remaining on this side of the mirror, she finds, in this story, it is a debt she does not necessarily owe to strangers. But in "Three Days and a Question," she tells about three strangers she met on the streets of New York— the man with an Auschwitz tattoo, the boy with AIDS, and the cab driver with black skin.

Even on this side, there always has to be more than one

story if it is to be told at all. In "Debts," one is the story of the stories, the other the story of Lucia's mother and grandmother and the man Michael whom her mother hated but had to care for when he became ill. In "Traveling," we read the story of the mother who refuses to change seats in the bus, and the story of the daughter, who, some years later, held a black child to relieve the standing mother. And, also, of course, the story of those stories, how the mother's story was transmitted to the writer years after her mother' death. And the story of her grandson, before she even knew about him. Within the story of Faith at home, "The Long-Distance Runner" intercalates the story of the African American community that has taken over her old neighborhood. "Three Days and a Question" makes one story and one question out of three: three encounters in three days, three repetitions of the same simple everyday gesture of pulling up a shirt sleeve. And "My Father Addresses Me on the Facts of Old Age," tells both the father-daughter conversation and the submerged non-conversation, the things they cannot discuss—her divorce, his intimate desires, his brother's political activities in Russia. Always two stories or more, playing off against each other, lighting each other, as does the work of Grace Paley and Robert Nichols in this volume. Reading both not only allows us to read each one of them differently, but also to read the world more optimistically, more lovingly, more humorously. And to talk to our hearts.[1]

NOTES

1. I would like to thank Grace Paley and Robert Nichols for their willingness to discuss their work with me in such generous and hospitable settings. Their friendship is a precious gift. I am grateful also to Sidra DeKoven Ezrahi, Jennifer James, Nancy K. Miller, Ivy Schweitzer, Leo Spitzer and Susan Winnett for invaluable suggestions on earlier drafts of this introduction.

WORKS CITED

Ezrahi, Sidra DeKoven. 2006. "Paley, Grace." In *The Greenwood Encyclopedia of American Poets and Poetry, Vol. 4*. Ed. Jeffrey Gray, James McCorkle, and Mary McAleer Balkun. Westport, CT, 1200–1.

Paley, Grace. 1998. *Just as I Thought*. New York: Farrar, Strauss and Giroux.

Women's World. 1994. "Feminist Organizing within International PEN," http://www.wworld.org/about/history.htm.

GRACE PALEY

THE LONG-DISTANCE RUNNER

—

One day, before or after forty-two, I became a long-distance runner. Though I was stout and in many ways inadequate to this desire, I wanted to go far and fast, not as fast as bicycles and trains, not as far as Taipei, Hingwen, places like that, islands of the slant-eyed cunt, as sailors in bus stations say when speaking of travel, but round and round the county from the seaside to the bridges, along the old neighborhood streets a couple of times, before old age and urban renewal ended them and me.

I tried the country first, Connecticut, which being wooded is always full of buds in spring. All creation is secret, isn't that true? So I trained in the wide-zoned suburban hills where I wasn't known. I ran all spring in and out of dogwood bloom, then laurel.

People sometimes stopped and asked me why I ran, a lady in silk shorts halfway down over her fat thighs. In training, I replied and rested only to answer if closely questioned. I wore a white sleeveless undershirt as well, with excellent support, not to attract the attention of old men and prudish children.

Then summer came, my legs seemed strong. I kissed the kids goodbye. They were quite old by then. It was near the time for parting anyway. I told Mrs. Raftery to look in now and then and give them some of that rotten Celtic supper she makes.

I told them they could take off any time they wanted to. Go lead your private life, I said. Only leave me out of it.

A word to the wise . . . said Richard.

You're depressed Faith, Mrs. Raftery said. Your boyfriend Jack, the one you think's so hotsy-totsy, hasn't called and you're as gloomy as a tick on Sunday.

Cut the folkshit with me, Raftery, I muttered. Her eyes filled with tears because that's who she is: folkshit from bunion to topknot. That's how she got liked by me, loved, invented, and endured.

When I walked out the door they were all reclining before the television set, Richard, Tonto, and Mrs. Raftery, gazing at the news. Which proved with moving pictures that there *had* been a voyage to the moon and Africa and South America hid in a furious whorl of clouds.

I said, Goodbye. They said, Yeah, O.K., sure.

If that's how it is, forget it, I hollered and took the Independent subway to Brighton Beach.

At Brighton Beach I stopped at the Salty Breezes Locker Room to change my clothes. Twenty-five years ago my father invested $500 in its future. In fact he still clears about $3.50 a year, which goes directly (by law) to the Children of Judea to cover their deficit.

No one paid too much attention when I started to run, easy and light on my feet. I ran on the boardwalk first, past my mother's leafleting station—between a soft-ice-cream

24

stand and a degenerated dune. There she had been assigned by her comrades to halt the tides of cruel American enterprise with simple socialist sense.

I wanted to stop and admire the long beach. I wanted to stop in order to think admiringly about New York. There aren't many rotting cities so tan and sandy and speckled with citizens at their salty edges. But I had already spent a lot of life lying down or standing and staring. I had decided to run.

After about a mile and a half I left the boardwalk and began to trot into the old neighborhood. I was running well. My breath was long and deep. I was thinking pridefully about my form.

Suddenly I was surrounded by about three hundred blacks.

Who you?

Who that?

Look at her! Just look! When you seen a fatter ass?

Poor thing. She ain't right. Leave her, you boys, you bad boys.

I used to live here, I said.

Oh yes, they said, in the white old days. That time too bad to last.

But we loved it here. We never went to Flatbush Avenue or Times Square. We loved our block.

Tough black titty.

I like your speech, I said. Metaphor and all.

Right on. We get that from talking.

Yes my people also had a way of speech. And don't forget the Irish. The gift of gab.

Who they? said a small boy.

Cops.

Nowadays, I suggested, there's more than Irish on the police force.

You right, said two ladies. More more, much much more. They's French Chinamen Russkies Congoleans. Oh missee, you too right.

I lived in that house, I said. That apartment house. All my life. Till I got married.

Now that *is* nice. Live in one place. My mother live that way in South Carolina. One place. Her daddy farmed. She said. They ate. No matter winter war bad times. Roosevelt. Something! Ain't that wonderful! And it weren't cold! Big trees!

That apartment. I looked up and pointed. There. The third floor.

They all looked up. So what! You blubrous devil! said a dark young man. He wore horn-rimmed glasses and had that intelligent look that City College boys used to have when I was eighteen and first looked at them.

He seemed to lead them in contempt and anger, even the littlest ones who moved toward me with dramatic stealth, singing, Devil, Oh Devil. I don't think the little kids had bad feeling because they poked a finger into me, then laughed.

Still I thought it might be wise to keep my head. So I jumped right in with some facts. I said, How many flowers' names do you know? Wildflowers, I mean. My people only knew two. That's what they say now anyway. Rich or poor, they only had two flowers' names. Rose and violet.

Daisy, said one boy immediately.

Weed, said another. That *is* a flower, I thought. But everyone else got the joke.

Saxifrage, lupine, said a lady. Viper's bugloss, said a small Girl Scout in medium green with a dark green sash. She held up a *Handbook of Wildflowers*.

How many you know, fat mama? a boy asked warmly. He wasn't against my being a mother or fat. I turned all my attention to him.

Oh sonny, I said, I'm way ahead of my people. I know in yellows alone: common cinquefoil, trout lily, yellow adder's-tongue, swamp buttercup and common buttercup, golden sorrel, yellow or hop clover, devil's-paintbrush, evening primrose, black-eyed Susan, golden aster, also the yellow pickerelweed growing down by the water if not in the water, and dandelions of course. I've seen all these myself. Seen them.

You could see China from the boardwalk, a boy said. When it's nice.

I know more flowers than countries. Mostly young people these days have traveled in many countries.

Not me. I ain't been nowhere.

Not me either, said about seventeen boys.

I'm not allowed, said a little girl. There's drunken junkies.

But *I! I!* cried out a tall black youth, very handsome and well dressed. I am an African. My father came from the high stolen plains. *I* have been everywhere. I was in Moscow six months, learning machinery. I was in France, learning French. I was in Italy, observing the peculiar Renaissance and the people's sweetness. I was in England, where I studied the common law and the urban blight. I was at the Conference of Dark Youth in Cuba to understand our passion. I am now here. Here am I to become an engineer and return to my people, around the Cape of Good Hope in a Norwegian sailing vessel. In this way I will learn the fine old art of sailing in case the engines of the new society of my old inland country should fail.

We had an extraordinary amount of silence after that. Then one old lady in a black dress and high white lace collar said to another old lady dressed exactly the same way, Glad tidings when someone got brains in the head not fish juice. Amen, said a few.

Whyn't you go up to Mrs. Luddy living in your house, you lady, huh? The Girl Scout asked this.

Why she just groove to see you, said some sarcastic snickerer.

She got palpitations. Her man, he give it to her.

That ain't all, he a natural gift-giver.

I'll take you, said the Girl Scout. My name is Cynthia. I'm in Troop 355, Brooklyn.

I'm not dressed, I said, looking at my lumpy knees.

You shouldn't wear no undershirt like that without no runnin number or no team writ on it. It look like a undershirt.

Cynthia! Don't take her up there, said an important boy. Her head strange. Don't you take her. Hear?

Lawrence, she said softly, you tell me once more what to do I'll wrap you round that lamppost.

Git! she said, powerfully addressing *me*.

In this way I was led into the hallway of the whole house of my childhood.

The first door I saw was still marked in flaky gold, 1A. That's where the janitor lived, I said. He was a Negro.

How come like that? Cynthia made an astonished face. How come the janitor was a black man?

Oh Cynthia, I said. Then I turned to the opposite door, first floor front, 1B. I remembered. Now, here, this was Mrs. Goreditsky, very very fat lady. All her children died at birth. Born, then one, two, three. Dead. Five children, then Mr. Goreditsky said, I'm bad luck on you Tessie and he went away. He sent $15 a week for seven years. Then no one heard.

I know her, poor thing, said Cynthia. The city come for her summer before last. The way they knew, it smelled. They wropped her up in a canvas. They couldn't get through the front door. It scraped off a piece of her. My Uncle Ronald had to help them, but he got disgusted.

Only two years ago. She was still here! Wasn't she scared?

So we all, said Cynthia. White ain't everything.

Who lived up here, she asked, 2B? Right now, my best

friend Nancy Rosalind lives here. She got two brothers, and her sister married and got a baby. She very light-skinned. Not her mother. We got all colors amongst us.

Your best friend? That's funny. Because it was *my* best friend. Right in that apartment. Joanna Rosen.

What become of her? Cynthia asked. She got a running shirt too?

Come on Cynthia, if you really want to know, I'll tell you. She married this man, Marvin Steirs.

Who's he?

I recollected his achievements. Well, he's the president of a big corporation, JoMar Plastics. This corporation owns a steel company, a radio station, a new Xerox-type machine that lets you do twenty-five different pages at once. This corporation has a foundation, The JoMar Fund for Research in Conservation. Capitalism is like that, I added, in order to be politically useful.

How come you know? You go over their house a lot?

No. I happened to read all about them on the financial page, just last week. It made me think: a different life. That's all.

Different spokes for different folks, said Cynthia.

I sat down on the cool marble steps and remembered Joanna's cousin Ziggie. He was older than we were. He wrote a poem which told us we were lovely flowers and our legs were petals, which nature would force open no matter how many times we said no.

Then I had several other interior thoughts that I couldn't

share with a child, the kind that give your face a blank or melancholy look.

Now you're not interested, said Cynthia. Now you're not gonna say a thing. Who lived here, 2A? Who? Two men lives here now. Women coming and women going. My mother says, Danger sign: Stay away, my darling, stay away.

I don't remember, Cynthia. I really don't.

You got to. What'd you come for, anyways?

Then I tried. 2A. 2A. Was it the twins? I felt a strong obligation as though remembering was in charge of the *existence* of the past. This is not so.

Cynthia, I said, I don't want to go any further. I don't even want to remember.

Come on, she said, tugging at my shorts, don't you want to see Mrs. Luddy, the one lives in your old house? That be fun, no?

No. No, I don't want to see Mrs. Luddy.

Now you shouldn't pay no attention to those boys downstairs. She will like you. I mean, she is kind. She don't like most white people, but she might like you.

No Cynthia, it's not that, but I don't want to see my father and mother's house now.

I don't know what to say. I said, Because my mother's dead. This was a lie, because my mother lives in her own room with my father in the Children of Judea. With her hand over her socialist heart, she reads the paper every morning after breakfast. Then she says sadly to my father, Every day the same. Dying . . . dying, dying from killing.

My mother's dead Cynthia. I can't go in there.

Oh . . . oh, the poor thing, she said, looking into my eyes. Oh, if my mother died, I don't know what I'd do. Even if I was old as you. I could kill myself. Tears filled her eyes and started down her cheeks. If my mother died, what would I do? She is my protector, she won't let the pushers get me. She hold me tight. She gonna hide me in the cedar box if my Uncle Rudford comes try to get me back. She *can't* die, my mother.

Cynthia—honey—she won't die. She's young. I put my arm out to comfort her. You could come live with me, I said. I got two boys, they're nearly grown up. I missed it, not having a girl.

What? What you mean now, live with you and boys. She pulled away and ran for the stairs. Stay away from me, honky lady. I know them white boys. They just gonna try and jostle my black womanhood. My mother told me about that, keep you white honky devil boys to your devil self, you just leave me be you old bitch you. Somebody help me, she started to scream, you hear. Somebody help. She gonna take me away.

She flattened herself to the wall, trembling. I was too frightened by her fear of me to say, Honey, I wouldn't hurt you, it's me. I heard her helpers, the voices of large boys crying, We coming, we coming, hold your head up, we coming. I ran past her fear to the stairs and up them two at a time. I came to my old own door. I knocked like the landlord, loud and terrible.

Mama not home, a child's voice said. No, no, I said.

32

It's me! a lady! Someone's chasing me, let me in. Mama not home, I ain't allowed to open up for nobody.

It's me! I cried out in terror. Mama! Mama! let me in!

The door opened. A slim woman whose age I couldn't invent looked at me. She said, Get in and shut that door tight. She took a hard pinching hold on my upper arm. Then she bolted the door herself. Them hustlers after you. They make me pink. Hide this white lady now, Donald. Stick her under your bed, you got a high bed.

Oh that's O.K. I'm fine now, I said. I felt safe and at home.

You in my house, she said. You do as I say. For two cents, I throw you out.

I squatted under a small kid's pissy mattress. Then I heard the knock. It was tentative and respectful. My mama don't allow me to open. Donald! someone called. Donald!

Oh no, he said. Can't do it. She gonna wear me out. You know her. She already tore up my ass this morning once. Ain't *gonna* open up.

I lived there for about three weeks with Mrs. Luddy and Donald and three little baby girls nearly the same age. I told her a joke about Irish twins. Ain't Irish, she said.

Nearly every morning the babies woke us at about 6:45. We gave them all a bottle and went back to sleep till 8:00. I made coffee and she changed diapers. Then it really stank for a while. At this time I usually said, Well listen, thanks really, but I've got to go I guess. I guess I'm going. She'd usually say, Well, guess again. *I* guess you ain't. Or if she was feeling disgusted she'd say, Go on now! Get! You wanna go, I guess by now I have snorted enough white lady stink to choke a horse. Go on!

I'd get to the door and then I'd hear voices. I'm ashamed to say I'd become fearful. Despite my wide geographical love of mankind, I would be attacked by local fears.

There was a sentimental truth that lay beside all that going and not going. It *was* my house where I'd lived long ago my family life. There was a tile on the bathroom floor that I myself had broken, dropping a hammer on the toe of my brother Charles as he stood dreamily shaving, his prick halfway up his undershorts. Astonishment and knowledge first seized me right there. The kitchen was the same. The table was the enameled table common to our class, easy to clean, with wooden undercorners for indigent and old cockroaches that couldn't make it to the kitchen sink. (However, it was not the same table, because I have inherited that one, chips and all.)

The living room was something like ours, only we had less plastic. There may have been less plastic in the world at that time. Also, my mother had set beautiful cushions everywhere, on beds and chairs. It was the way she expressed herself, artistically, to embroider at night or take strips of flowered cotton and sew them across ordinary white or blue muslin in the most delicate designs, the way women have always used materials that live and die in hunks and tatters to say: This is my place.

Mrs. Luddy said, Uh huh!

Of course, I said, men don't have that outlet. That's how come they run around so much.

Till they drunk enough to lay down, she said.

Yes, I said, on a large scale you can see it in the world. First they make something, then they murder it. Then they write a book about how interesting it is.

You got something there, she said. Sometimes she said, Girl, you don't know *nothing*.

We often sat at the window looking out and down. Little tufts of breeze grew on that windowsill. The blazing afternoon was around the corner and up the block.

You say men, she said. Is that men? she asked. What you call—a Man?

Four flights below us, leaning on the stoop, were about a dozen people and around them devastation. Just a minute, I said. I had seen devastation on my way, running, gotten some of the pebbles of it in my running shoe and the dust of it in my eyes. I had thought with the indignant courtesy of a citizen, This is a disgrace to the City of New York, which I love and am running through.

But now, from the commanding heights of home, I saw it clearly. The tenement in which Jack my old and present friend had come to gloomy manhood had been destroyed, first by fire, then by demolition (which is a swinging ball of steel that cracks bedrooms and kitchens). Because of this work, we could see several blocks wide and a block and a half long. That weird guy Eddy—his house still stood, famous

1510 gutted, with black window frames, no glass, open laths. The stubbornness of the supporting beams! Some persons or families still lived on the lowest floors. In the lots between, a couple of old sofas lay on their fat faces, their springs sticking up into the air. Just as in wartime a half dozen ailanthus trees had already found their first quarter inch of earth and begun a living attack on the dead yards. At night, I knew animals roamed the place, squalling and howling, furious New York dogs and street cats and mighty rats. You would think you were in Bear Mountain Park, the terror of venturing forth.

Someone ought to clean that up, I said.

Mrs. Luddy said, Who you got in mind? Mrs. Kennedy?—

Donald made a stern face. He said, That just what I gonna do when I get big. Gonna get the Sanitary Man in and show it to him. You see that, you big guinea you, you clean it up right now! Then he stamped his feet and fierced his eyes.

Mrs. Luddy said, Come here, you little nigger. She kissed the top of his head and gave him a whack on the backside all at one time.

Well, said Donald, encouraged, look out there now you all! Go on I say, look! Though we had already seen, to please him we looked. On the stoop men and boys lounged, leaned, hopped about, stood on one leg, then another, took their socks off, and scratched their toes, talked, sat on their haunches, heads down, dozing.

Donald said, Look at them. They ain't got self-respect.

They got Afros *on* their heads, but they don't know they black *in* their heads.

I thought he ought to learn to be more sympathetic. I said, There are reasons that people are that way.

Yes, ma'am, said Donald.

Anyway, how come you never go down and play with the other kids, how come you're up here so much?

My mama don't like me do that. Some of them is bad. Bad. I might become a dope addict. I got to stay clear.

You just a dope, that's a fact, said Mrs. Luddy.

He ought to be with kids his age more, I think.

He see them in school, miss. Don't trouble your head about it if you don't mind.

Actually, Mrs. Luddy didn't go down into the street either. Donald did all the shopping. She let the welfare investigator in, the meterman came into the kitchen to read the meter. I saw him from the back room, where I hid. She did pick up her check. She cashed it. She returned to wash the babies, change their diapers, wash clothes, iron, feed people, and then in free half hours she sat by that window. She was waiting.

I believed she was watching and waiting for a particular man. I wanted to discuss this with her, talk lovingly like sisters. But before I could freely say, Forget about the son of a bitch, he's a pig, I did have to offer a few solid facts about myself, my kids, about fathers, husbands, passersby, evening companions, and the life of my father and mother in this room by this exact afternoon window.

I told her, for instance, that in my worst times I had given myself one extremely simple physical pleasure. This was cream cheese for breakfast. In fact, I insisted on it, sometimes depriving the children of very important articles and food.

Girl, you don't know nothing, she said.

Then for a little while she talked gently as one does to a person who is innocent and insane and incorruptible because of stupidity. She had had two such special pleasures for hard times, she said. The first, men, but they turned rotten, white women had ruined the best, give them the idea their dicks made of solid gold. The second pleasure she had tried was wine. She said, I do like wine. You *has* to have something just for yourself by yourself. Then she said, But you can't raise a decent boy when you liquor-dazed every night.

White or black, I said, returning to men, they did think they were bringing a rare gift, whereas it was just sex, which is common like bread, though essential.

Oh, you can do without, she said. There's folks does without.

I told her Donald deserved the best. I loved him. If he had flaws, I hardly noticed them. It's one of my beliefs that children do not have flaws, even the worst do not.

Donald was brilliant—like my boys except that he had an easier disposition. For this reason I decided, almost the second moment of my residence in that household, to bring him up to reading level at once. I told him we would work with books and newspapers. He went immediately to his neighborhood library and brought some hard books to amuse me. *Black Folktales* by Julius Lester and *The Pushcart War*, which is about another neighborhood but relevant.

Donald always agreed with me when we talked about reading and writing. In fact, when I mentioned poetry, he told me he knew all about it, that David Henderson, a known black poet, had visited his second-grade class. So Donald was, as it turned out, well ahead of my nosy tongue. He was usually very busy shopping. He also had to spend a lot of time making faces to force the little serious baby girls into laughter. But if the subject came up, he could take *the* poem right out of the air into which language and event had just gone.

An example: That morning, his mother had said, Whew, I just got too much piss and diapers and wash. I wanna just sit down by that window and rest myself. He wrote a poem:

> *Just got too much pissy diapers*
> *and wash and wash*
> *just wanna sit down by that window*
> *and look out*
>   *ain't nothing there.*

Donald, I said, you are plain brilliant. I'm never going to forget you. For godsakes don't you forget me.

You fool with him too much, said Mrs. Luddy. He already don't even remember his grandma, you never gonna meet someone like her, a curse never come past her lips.

I do remember, Mama, I remember. She lying in bed,

right there. A man standing in the door. She say, Esdras, I put a curse on you head. You worsen tomorrow. How come she said like that?

Gomorrah, I believe Gomorrah, she said. She know the Bible inside out.

Did she live with you?

No. No, she visiting. She come up to see us all, her children, how we doing. She come up to see sights. Then she lay down and died. She was old.

I remained quiet because of the death of mothers. Mrs. Luddy looked at me thoughtfully, then she said:

My mama had stories to tell, she raised me on. *Her* mama was a little thing, no sense. Stand in the door of the cabin all day, sucking her thumb. It was slave times. One day a young field boy come storming along. He knock on the door of the first cabin hollering, Sister, come out, it's freedom. She come out. She say, Yeah? When? He say, Now! It's freedom now! Then he knock at the next door and say, Sister! It's freedom! Now! From one cabin he run to the next cabin, crying out, Sister, it's freedom now!

Oh I remember that story, said Donald. Freedom now! Freedom now! He jumped up and down.

You don't remember nothing boy. Go on, get Eloise, she want to get into the good times.

Eloise was two but undersized. We got her like that, said Donald. Mrs. Luddy let me buy her ice cream and green vegetables. She was waiting for kale and chard, but it was too early. The kale liked cold. You not about to be here

40

November, she said. No, no. I turned away, lonesomeness touching me, and sang our Eloise song:

Eloise loves the bees
the bees they buzz
like Eloise does.

Then Eloise crawled all over the splintery floor, buzzing wildly.

Oh you crazy baby, said Donald, buzz buzz buzz.

Mrs. Luddy sat down by the window.

You all make a lot of noise, she said sadly. You just right on noisy.

The next morning Mrs. Luddy woke me up.

Time to go, she said.

What?

Home.

What? I said.

Well, don't you think your little spoiled boys crying for you? Where's Mama? They standing in the window. Time to go lady. This ain't Free Vacation Farm. Time we was by ourself a little.

Oh Ma, said Donald, she ain't a lot of trouble. Go on, get Eloise, she hollering. And button up your lip.

She didn't offer me coffee. She looked at me strictly all the time. I tried to look strictly back, but I failed because I loved the sight of her.

Donald was teary, but I didn't dare turn my face to him,

41

until the parting minute at the door. Even then, I kissed the top of his head a little too forcefully and said, Well, I'll see you.

On the front stoop there were about half a dozen mid-morning family people and kids arguing about who had dumped garbage out of which window. They were very disgusted with one another.

Two young men in handsome dashikis stood in counsel and agreement at the street corner. They divided a comment. How come white womens got rotten teeth? And look so old? A young woman waiting at the light said, Hush . . .

I walked past them and didn't begin my run till the road opened up somewhere along Ocean Parkway. I was a little stiff because my way of life had used only small movements, an occasional stretch to put a knife or teapot out of reach of the babies. I ran about ten, fifteen blocks. Then my second wind came, which is classical, famous among runners, it's the beginning of flying.

In the three weeks I'd been off the street, jogging had become popular. It seemed that I was only one person doing her thing, which happened like most American eccentric acts to be the most "in" thing I could have done. In fact, two young men ran alongside of me for nearly a mile. They ran silently beside me and turned off at Avenue H. A gentleman with a mustache, running poorly in the opposite direction, waved. He called out, Hi, señora.

Near home I ran through our park, where I had aired my children on weekends and late-summer afternoons. I stopped at the northeast playground, where I met a dozen young mothers intelligently handling their little ones. In order to prepare them, meaning no harm, I said, In fifteen years, you girls will be like me, wrong in everything.

At home it was Saturday morning. Jack had returned looking as grim as ever, but he'd brought cash and a vacuum cleaner. While the coffee perked, he showed Richard how to use it. They were playing ticktacktoe on the dusty wall.

Richard said, Well! Look who's here! Hi!

Any news? I asked.

Letter from Daddy, he said. From the lake and water country in Chile. He says it's like Minnesota.

He's never been to Minnesota, I said. Where's Anthony?

Here I am, said Tonto, appearing. But I'm leaving.

Oh yes, I said. Of course. Every Saturday he hurries through breakfast or misses it. He goes to visit his friends in institutions. These are well-known places like Bellevue, Hillside, Rockland State, Central Islip, Manhattan. These visits take him all day and sometimes half the night.

I found some chocolate-chip cookies in the pantry. Take them, Tonto, I said. I remember nearly all his friends as little boys and girls always hopping, skipping, jumping, and cookie-eating. He was annoyed. He said, No! Chocolate cookies is what the commissaries are full of. How about money?

Jack dropped the vacuum cleaner. He said, No! They have parents for that.

I said, Here, five dollars for cigarettes, one dollar each.

Cigarettes! said Jack. Goddamnit! Black lungs and death! Cancer! Emphysema! He stomped out of the kitchen, breathing. He took the bike from the back room and started for Central Park, which has been closed to cars but opened to bicycle riders. When he'd been gone about ten minutes, Anthony said, It's really open only on Sundays.

Why didn't you say so? Why can't you be decent to him? I asked. It's important to me.

Oh Faith, he said, patting me on the head because he'd grown so tall, all that air. It's good for his lungs. And his muscles! He'll be back soon.

You should ride too, I said. You don't want to get mushy in your legs. You should go swimming once a week.

I'm too busy, he said. I have to see my friends.

Then Richard, who had been vacuuming under his bed, came into the kitchen. You still here, Tonto?

Going going gone, said Anthony, don't bat your eye.

Now listen, Richard said, here's a note. It's for Judy, if you get as far as Rockland. Don't forget it. Don't open it. Don't read it. I know he'll read it.

Anthony smiled and slammed the door.

Did I lose weight? I asked. Yes, said Richard. You look O.K. You never look too bad. But where were you? I got sick of Raftery's boiled potatoes. Where were you, Faith?

Well! I said. Well! I stayed a few weeks in my old apartment, where Grandpa and Grandma and me and Hope and Charlie lived, when we were little. I took you there long ago. Not so far from the ocean where Grandma made us very healthy with sun and air.

What are you talking about? said Richard. Cut the baby talk.

Anthony came home earlier than expected that evening because some people were in shock therapy and someone else had run away. He listened to me for a while. Then he said, I don't know what she's talking about either.

Neither did Jack, despite the understanding often produced by love after absence. He said, Tell me again. He was in a good mood. He said, You can even tell it to me twice.

I repeated the story. They all said, What?

Because it isn't usually so simple. Have you known it to happen much nowadays? A woman inside the steamy energy of middle age runs and runs. She finds the houses and streets where her childhood happened. She lives in them. She learns as though she was still a child what in the world is coming next.

HERE

—

Here I am in the garden laughing
an old woman with heavy breasts
and a nicely mapped face

how did this happen
well that's who I wanted to be

at last   a woman
in the old style   sitting
stout thighs apart under
a big skirt   grandchild sliding
on   off my lap   a pleasant
summer perspiration

that's my old man across the yard
he's talking to the meter reader
he's telling him the world's sad story
how electricity is oil or uranium
and so forth   I tell my grandson
run over to your grandpa   ask him
to sit beside me for a minute   I
am suddenly exhausted by my desire
to kiss his sweet explaining lips

ANTI-LOVE POEM

—

Sometimes you don't want to love the person you love
you turn your face away from that face
whose eyes lips might make you give up anger
forget insult   steal sadness of not wanting
to love   turn away then turn away   at breakfast
in the evening don't lift your eyes from the paper
to see that face in all its seriousness a
sweetness of concentration   he holds his book
in his hand   the hard-knuckled winter wood-
scarred fingers   turn away   that's all you can
do old as you are to save yourself from love

DEBTS

A lady called me up today. She said she was in possession
of her family archives. She had heard I was a writer. She
wondered if I would help her write about her grandfather,
a famous innovator and dreamer of the Yiddish theater. I
said I had already used every single thing I knew about the
Yiddish theater to write one story, and I didn't have time
to learn any more, then write about it. There is a long time
in me between knowing and telling. She offered a share of
the profits, but that is something too inorganic. It would
never rush her grandfather's life into any literature I could
make.

The next day, my friend Lucia and I had coffee and
we talked about this woman. Lucia explained to me that
it was probably hard to have family archives or even only
stories about outstanding grandparents or uncles when one
was sixty or seventy and there was no writer in the family
and the children were in the middle of their own lives. She
said it was a pity to lose all this inheritance just because of
one's own mortality. I said yes, I did understand. We drank
more coffee. Then I went home.

I thought about our conversation. Actually, I owed
nothing to the lady who'd called. It was possible that I did
owe something to my own family and the families of my

friends. That is, to tell their stories as simply as possible, in order, you might say, to save a few lives.

Because it was her idea, the first story is Lucia's. I tell it so that some people will remember Lucia's grandmother, also her mother, who in this story is eight or nine.

The grandmother's name was Maria. The mother's name was Anna. They lived on Mott Street in Manhattan in the early 1900s. Maria was married to a man named Michael. He had worked hard, but bad luck and awful memories had driven him to the Hospital for the Insane on Welfare Island.

Every morning Anna took the long trip by trolley and train and trolley again to bring him his hot dinner. He could not eat the meals at the hospital. When Anna rode out of the stone streets of Manhattan over the bridge to the countryside of Welfare Island, she was always surprised. She played for a long time on the green banks of the river. She picked wildflowers in the fields, and then she went up to the men's ward.

One afternoon, she arrived as usual. Michael felt very weak and asked her to lean on his back and support him while he sat at the edge of the bed eating dinner. She did so, and that is how come, when he fell back and died, it was in her thin little arms that he lay. He was very heavy. She held him so, just for a minute or two, then let him fall to the bed. She told an orderly and went home. She didn't cry because she didn't like him. She spoke first to a neighbor, and then together they told her mother.

Now this is the main part of the story:

The man Michael was not her father. Her father had died when she was little. Maria, with the other small children, had tried to live through the hard times in the best way. She moved in with different, nearly related families in the neighborhood and worked hard helping out in their houses. She worked well, and it happened that she was also known for the fine bread she baked. She would live in a good friend's house for a while baking magnificent bread. But soon, the husband of the house would say, "Maria bakes wonderful bread. Why can't you learn to bake bread like that?" He would probably then seem to admire her in other ways. Wisely, the wife would ask Maria to please find another home.

One day at the spring street festival, she met a man named Michael, a relative of friends. They couldn't marry because Michael had a wife in Italy. In order to live with him, Maria explained the following truths to her reasonable head:

1. This man Michael was tall with a peculiar scar on his shoulder. Her husband had been unusually tall and had had a scar on his shoulder.
2. This man was redheaded. Her dead husband had been redheaded.
3. This man was a tailor. Her husband had been a tailor.
4. His name was Michael. Her husband had been called Michael.

In this way, persuading her own understanding, Maria was able to not live alone at an important time in her life, to have a father for the good of her children's character, a man in her bed for comfort, a husband to serve. Still and all, though he died in her arms, Anna, the child, didn't like him at all. It was a pity, because he had always called her "my little one." Every day she had visited him, she had found him in the hallway waiting, or at the edge of his white bed, and she had called out, "Hey, Zio, here's your dinner. Mama sent it. I have to go now."

THREE DAYS AND A QUESTION

—

On the first day I joined a demonstration opposing the arrest in Israel of members of Yesh Gvul, Israeli soldiers who had refused to serve in the occupied territories. Yesh Gvul means: *There is a Limit*.

TV cameras and an anchorwoman arrived and *New York Times* stringers with their narrow journalism notebooks. What do you think? the anchorwoman asked. What do *you* think, she asked a woman passer-by—a woman about my age.

Anti-Semites, the woman said quietly.

The anchorwoman said, But they're Jewish.

Anti-Semites, the woman said, a little louder.

What? One of our demonstrators stepped up to her. Are you crazy? How can you . . . Listen what we're saying.

Rotten anti-Semites—all of you.

What? What What the man shouted. How you dare to say that—all of us Jews. Me, he said. He pulled up his shirt-sleeves. Me? You call me? You look. He held out his arm. Look at this.

I'm not looking, she screamed.

You look at my number, what they did to me. My arm . . . you have no right.

Anti-Semite, she said between her teeth. Israel hater.

No, no he said, you fool. My arm—you're afraid to look . . . my arm . . . my arm.

On the second day Vera and I listen at PEN to Eta Krisaeva read her stories that were not permitted publication in her own country, Czechoslovakia. Then we walk home in the New York walking night, about twenty blocks—shops and lights, other walkers talking past us. Late-night homeless men and women asleep in dark storefront doorways on cardboard pallets under coats and newspapers, scraps of blanket. Near home on Sixth Avenue a young man, a boy, passes—a boy the age a younger son could be—head down, bundles in his arms, on his back.

Wait, he says, turning to stop us. Please, please wait. I just got out of Bellevue. I was sick. They gave me something. I don't know . . . I need to sleep somewhere. The Y, maybe.

That's way uptown.

Yes, he says. He looks at us. Carefully he says, AIDS. He looks away. Oh. Separately, Vera and I think: A boy—only a boy. Mothers after all, our common trade for more than thirty years.

Then he says, I put out my hand. We think he means to tell us he tried to beg. I put out my hand. No one will help me. No one. Because they can see. Look at my arm. He pulls his coatsleeve back. Lesions, he says. Have you ever seen lesions? That's what people see.

No. No, we see a broad fair forehead, a pale countenance, fear. I just have to sleep, he says.

We shift in our pockets. We give him what we find—about eight dollars. We tell him, Son, they'll help you on 13th Street at the Center. Yes, I know about that place. I know about them all. He hoists the bundle of his things to his back to prepare for walking. Thank you, ladies. Goodbye.

On the third day I'm in a taxi. I'm leaving the city for a while and need to get to the airport. We talk—the driver and I. He's a black man, dark. He's not young. He has a French accent. Where are you from? Haiti, he answers. Ah, your country is in bad trouble. Very bad. You know that, Miss.

Well, yes. Sometimes it's in the paper.

They thieves there. You know that? Very rich, very poor. You believe me? Killing—it's nothing to them, killing. Hunger. Starving people. Everything bad. And you don't let us come. Starving. They send us back.

We're at a red light. He turns to look at me. Why they do that? He doesn't wait for me to say, Well . . . because . . . He says, Why hard.

The light changes. We move slowly up traffic-jammed Third Avenue. Silence. Then, Why? Why they let the Nicaragua people come? Why they let Vietnamese come? One time American people want to kill them people. Put bomb in their children. Break their head. Now they say, Yes Yes, come come come. Not us. Why?

Your New York is beautiful country. I love it. So beautiful, this New York. But why, tell me, he says, stopping the cab, switching the meter off. Why, he says, turning to me again, rolling his short shirtsleeve back, raising his arm to the passenger divider, pinching and pulling the bare skin of his upper arm. You tell me—this skin, this black skin—why? Why you hate this skin so much?

Question: Those gestures, those arms, the three consecutive days thrown like a formal net over the barest unchanged accidental facts. How? Why? In order to become—probably—in this city one story told.

IS THERE A DIFFERENCE BETWEEN
MEN AND WOMEN

—

Oh the slave trade
    the arms trade
death on the high seas
    massacre in the villages

      trade in the markets
        melons mustard greens
    cloth shining dipped in
        onion dye beet grass
    trade in the markets   fish
        oil   yams   coconuts   leaves
    of water spinach   leaves
        of pure water   cucumbers
    pickled walking back
        and forth along the stalls
    cloth bleached to ivory
        argument from stall to stall
    disgusted and delighted
        in the market

oh the worldwide arms trade
    the trade in woman's bodies

the slave trade
    slaughter

            oranges coming in from
                the country in one
            basket on the long
                pole   coconuts in
            the other   on the
                shoulders of women
            walking   knees slightly bent
                scuffing   stumbling
            along the road   bringing
                rice into the city
            hoisting the bundles of dry
                mangrove for repair
            of the household   trade
                in the markets on
            the women's backs and shoulders
                yams   sometimes peanuts

oh the slave trade
    the trade in the bodies of women
the worldwide unending arms trade
    everywhere man-made slaughter

TRAVELING

—

My mother and sister were traveling south. The year was 1927. They had begun their journey in New York. They were going to visit my brother, who was studying in the South Medical College of Virginia. Their bus was an express and had stopped only in Philadelphia, Wilmington, and now Washington. Here, the darker people who had gotten on in Philadelphia or New York rose from their seats, put their bags and boxes together, and moved to the back of the bus. People who boarded in Washington knew where to seat themselves. My mother had heard that something like this would happen. My sister had heard of it, too. They had not lived in it. This reorganization of passengers by color happened in silence. My mother and sister remained in their seats, which were about three-quarters of the way back.

When everyone was settled, the bus driver began to collect tickets. My sister saw him coming. She pinched my mother: Ma! Look! Of course, my mother saw him, too. What frightened my sister was the quietness. The white people in front, the black people in back—silent.

The driver sighed, said, You can't sit here, ma'am. It's for them, waving over his shoulder at the Negroes, among whom they were now sitting. Move, please.

My mother said, No.

He said, You don't understand, ma'am. It's against the law. You have to move to the front.

My mother said, No.

When I first tried to write this scene, I imagined my mother saying, That's all right, mister, we're comfortable. I can't change my seat every minute. I read this invention to my sister. She said it was nothing like that. My mother did not try to be friendly or pretend innocence. While my sister trembled in the silence, my mother said, for the third time, quietly, No.

Somehow finally, they were in Richmond. There was my brother in school among so many American boys. After hugs and my mother's anxious looks at her young son, my sister said, Vic, you know what Mama did?

My brother remembers thinking, What? Oh! She wouldn't move? He had a classmate, a Jewish boy like himself, but from Virginia, who had had a public confrontation with a Negro man. He had punched that man hard, knocked him down. My brother couldn't believe it. He was stunned. He couldn't imagine a Jewish boy wanting to knock anyone down. He had never wanted to. But he thought, looking back, that he had been set down to work and study in a nearly foreign place and had to get used to it. Then he told me about the Second World War, when the disgrace of black soldiers being forced to sit behind white German POWs shook him. Shamed him.

About fifteen years later, in 1943, in early summer, I rode the bus for about three days from New York to Miami Beach, where my husband in sweaty fatigues, along with hundreds of other boys, was trudging up and down the streets and beaches to prepare themselves for war.

By late afternoon of the second long day, we were well into the South, beyond Richmond, maybe South Carolina or Georgia. My excitement about travel in the wide world was damaged a little by a sudden fear that I might not recognize Jess or he, me. We hadn't seen each other for two months. I took a photograph out of my pocket; yes, I would know him.

I had been sleeping waking reading writing dozing waking. So many hours, the movement of the passengers was something like a tide that sometimes ebbed and now seemed to be noisily rising. I opened my eyes to the sound of new people brushing past my aisle seat. And looked up to see a colored woman holding a large sleeping baby, who, with the heaviness of sleep, his arms so tight around her neck, seemed to be pulling her head down. I looked around and noticed that I was in the last white row. The press of travelers had made it impossible for her to move farther back. She seemed so tired and I had been sitting and sitting for a day and a half at least. Not thinking, or maybe refusing to think, I offered her my seat.

She looked to the right and left as well as she could. Softly she said, Oh no. I became fully awake. A white man was standing right beside her, but on the other side of the invisible absolute racial border. Of course, she couldn't accept my seat. Her sleeping child hung mercilessly from her neck. She shifted a little to balance the burden. She whispered to herself, Oh, I just don't know. So I said, Well, at least give me the baby. First, she turned, barely looking at the man beside her. He made no move. So, to my surprise, but obviously out of sheer exhaustion, she disengaged the child from her body and placed him on my lap. He was deep in child-sleep. He stirred, but not enough to bother himself or me. I liked holding him, aligning him along my twenty-year-old young woman's shape. I thought ahead to that holding, that breathing together that would happen in my life if this war would ever end.

I was so comfortable under his nice weight. I closed my eyes for a couple of minutes, but suddenly opened them to look up into the face of a white man talking. In a loud voice he addressed me: Lady, I wouldn't of touched that thing with a meat hook.

I thought, Oh, this world will end in ice. I could do nothing but look straight into his eyes. I did not look away from him. Then I held that boy a little tighter, kissed his curly head, pressed him even closer so that he began to squirm. So sleepy, he reshaped himself inside my arms. His mother tried to narrow herself away from that dangerous border, too frightened at first to move at all. After a couple of minutes, she leaned forward a little, placed her hand on the baby's head, and held it there until the next stop. I couldn't look up into her mother face.

I write this remembrance more than fifty years later. I look back at that mother and child. How young she is. Her hand on his head is quite small, though she tries by spreading her fingers wide to hide him from the white man. But the child I'm holding, his little face as he turns toward me, is the brown face of my own grandson, my daughter's boy, the open mouth of the sleeper, the full lips, the thick little body of a child who runs wildly from one end of the yard to the other, leaps from dangerous heights with certain experienced caution, muscling his body, his mind, for coming realities.

Of course, when my mother and sister returned from Richmond, the family at home wanted to know: How was Vic doing in school among all those gentiles? Was the long bus ride hard, was the anti-Semitism really bad or just normal? What happened on the bus? I was probably present at that supper, the attentive listener and total forgetter of information that immediately started to form me.

Then last year, my sister, casting the net of old age (through which recent experience easily slips), brought up that old story. First I was angry. How come you never told me about your bus ride with Mama? I mean, really, so many years ago.

I don't know, she said, anyway you were only about four years old, and besides, maybe I did.

I asked my brother why we'd never talked about that day. He said he thought now that it had had a great effect on him; he had tried unraveling its meaning for years—then life family work happened. So I imagined him, a youngster really, a kid from the Bronx in Virginia in 1927; why, he was a stranger there himself.

In the next couple of weeks, we continued to talk about our mother, the way she was principled, adamant, and at the same time so shy. What else could we remember . . . Well, I said, I have a story about those buses, too. Then I told it to them: How it happened on just such a journey, when I was still quite young, that I first knew my grandson, first held him close, but could protect him for only about twenty minutes fifty years ago.

IN THE BUS

Somewhere between Greenfield and Holyoke
snow became rain
and a child passed through me
as a person moves through mist
as the moon moves through
a dense cloud at night
as though I were cloud or mist
a child passed through me

On the highway that lies
across miles of stubble
and tobacco barns our bus speeding
speeding disordered the slanty rain
and a girl with no name   naked
wearing the last nakedness of
childhood   breathed in me
            once   no
            two breaths
a sigh   she whispered   Hey you
begin again
            Again?
again   again   you'll see
it's easy   begin again   long ago

MY FATHER ADDRESSES ME ON THE FACTS OF OLD AGE

—

My father had decided to teach me how to grow old. I said O.K. My children didn't think it was such a great idea. If I knew how, they thought, I might do so too easily. No, no, I said, it's for later, years from now. And, besides, if I get it right it might be helpful to you kids in time to come.

They said, Really?

My father wanted to begin as soon as possible. For God's sake, he said, you can talk to the kids later. Now, listen to me, send them out to play. You are so distractable.

We should probably begin at the beginning, he said. Change. First there is change, which nobody likes—even men. You'd be surprised. You can do little things—putting cream on the corners of your mouth, also the heels of your feet. But here is the main thing. Oh, I wish your mother was alive—not that she had time—

But Pa, I said, Mama never knew anything about cream. I did not say she was famous for not taking care.

Forget it, he said sadly. But I must mention squinting. DON'T SQUINT. Wear your glasses. Look at your aunt, so beautiful once. I know someone has said men don't make passes at girls who wear glasses, but that's an idea for a foolish person. There are many handsome women who are not exactly twenty-twenty.

Please sit down, he said. Be patient. The main thing is this—when you get up in the morning you must take your heart in your two hands. You must do this every morning.

That's a metaphor, right?

Metaphor? No, no, you can do this. In the morning, do a few little exercises for the joints, not too much. Then put your hands like a cup over and under the heart. Under the breast. He said tactfully. It's probably easier for a man. Then talk softly, don't yell. Under your ribs, push a little. When you wake up, you must do this massage. I mean pat, stroke a little, don't be ashamed. Very likely no one will be watching. Then you must talk to your heart.

Talk? What?

Say anything, but be respectful. Say—maybe say, Heart, little heart, beat softly but never forget your job, the blood. You can whisper also, Remember, remember. For instance, I said to it yesterday, Heart, heart, do you remember my brother, Grisha, how he made work for you that day when he came to the store and he said, Your boss's money, Zenya, right now? How he put a gun in my face and I said, Grisha, are you crazy? Why don't you ask me at home? I would give you. We were in this America not more than two years. He was only a kid. And he said, he said, Who needs your worker's money? For the movement—only from your boss. O little heart, you worked like a bastard, like a dog, like a crazy slave, bang, bang, bang that day, remember? That's the story I told my heart yesterday, my father said. What a racket it made to answer me, I remember, I remember, till I was dizzy with the thumping.

Why'd you do that, Pa? I don't get it.

Don't you see? This is good for the old heart—to get excited—just as good as for the person. Some people go running till late in life—for the muscles, they say, but the heart knows the real purpose. The purpose is the expansion of the arteries, a river of blood, it cleans off the banks, carries junk out of the system. I myself would rather remind the heart how frightened I was by my brother than go running in a strange neighborhood, miles and miles, with the city so dangerous these days.

I said, Oh, but then I said, Well, thanks.

I don't think you listened, he said. As usual—probably worried about the kids. They're not babies, you know. If you were better organized you wouldn't have so many worries.

I stopped by a couple of weeks later. This time he was annoyed.

Why did you leave the kids home? If you keep doing this, they'll forget who I am. Children are like old people in that respect.

They won't forget you, Pa, never in a million years.

You think so? God has not been so good about a million years. His main interest in us began—actually, he put it down in writing fifty-six, fifty-seven hundred years ago. In the Book. You know our Book, I suppose.

O.K. Yes.

Probably a million years is too close to his lifetime, if

you could call it life, what he goes through. I believe he said several times—when he was still in contact with us—I am a jealous God. Here and there he makes an exception. I read there are three-thousand-year-old trees somewhere in some godforsaken place. Of course, that's how come they're still alive. We should all be so godforsaken.

But no more joking around. I have been thinking what to tell you now. First of all, soon, maybe in twenty, thirty years, you'll begin to get up in the morning—4, 5 A.M. In a farmer that's O.K., but for us—you'll remember everything you did, didn't, what you omitted, whom you insulted, betrayed—betrayed, that is the worst. Do you remember, you didn't go see your aunt, she was dying? That will be on your mind like a stone. Of course, I myself did not behave so well. Still, I was so busy those days, long office hours, remember it was usual in those days for doctors to make house calls. No elevators, fourth floor, fifth floor, even in a nice Bronx tenement. But this morning, I mean *this* morning, a few hours ago, my mother, your babushka, came into my mind, looked at me.

Have I told you I was arrested? Of course I did. I was arrested a few times, but this time for some reason the policeman walked me past the office of the local jail. My mama was there, I saw her through the window. She was bringing me a bundle of clean clothes. She put it on the officer's table. She turned. She saw me. She looked at me through the glass with such a face, eye-to-eye. Despair. No hope. This morning, 4 A.M., I saw once more how she sat there, very straight. Her eyes. Because of that look, I did my term, my sentence, the best I could. I finished up six months in Arkhangel'sk, where they finally sent me. Then no more, no more, I said to myself, no more saving Imperial Russia, the great pogrom-maker, from itself.

Oh, Pa.

Don't make too much out of everything. Well, anyway, I want to tell you also how the body is your enemy. I must warn you it is not your friend the way it was when you were a youngster. For example. Greens—believe me—are over-rated. Some people believe they will cure cancer. It's the style. My experience with maybe a hundred patients proves otherwise. Greens are helpful to God. That fellow Sandburg, the poet—I believe from Chicago—explained it. Grass tip-toes over the whole world, holds it in place—except the desert, of course, everything there is loose, flying around.

How come you bring up God so much? When I was a kid you were a strict atheist, you even spit on the steps of the synagogue.

Well, God is very good for conversation, he said. By the way, I believe I have to tell you a few words about the stock market. Your brother-in-law is always talking about how brilliant he is, investing, investing. My advice to you: Stay out of it.

But people *are* making money. A lot. Read the paper. Even kids are becoming millionaires.

But what of tomorrow? he asked.

Tomorrow, I said, they'll make another million.

No, no, no, I mean TOMORROW. I was there when TO-MORROW came in 1929. So I say to them and their millions, HA HA HA, TOMORROW will come. Go home now, I have a great deal more to tell you. Somehow, I'm always tired.

I'll go in a minute—but I have to tell you something, Pa. I had to tell him that my husband and I were separating. Maybe even divorce, the first in the family.

What? What? Are you crazy? I don't understand you people nowadays. I married your mother when I was a boy. It's true I had a first-class mustache, but I was a kid, and you know I stayed married till the end. Once or twice, she wanted to part company, but not me. The reason, of course, she was inclined to be jealous.

He then gave me the example I'd heard five or six times before. What it was, one time two couples went to the movies. Arzemich and his wife, you remember. Well, I sat next to his wife, the lady of the couple, by the way a very attractive woman, and during the show, which wasn't so great, we talked about this and that, laughed a couple times. When we got home, your mother said, O.K. Anytime you want, right now, I'll give you a divorce. We will go our separate ways. Naturally, I said, What? Are you ridiculous?

My advice to you—stick it out. It's true your husband, he's a peculiar fellow, but think it over. Go home. Maybe you can manage at least till old age. Then, if you still don't get along, you can go to separate old-age homes.

Pa, it's no joke. It's my life.

It is a joke. A joke is necessary at this time. But I'm tired.

You'll see, in thirty, forty years from now, you'll get tired often. It doesn't mean you're sick. This is something important that I'm telling you. Listen. To live a long time, long years, you've got to sleep a certain extra percentage away. It's a shame.

It was at least three weeks before I saw him again. He was drinking tea, eating a baked apple, one of twelve my sister baked for him every ten days. I took another one out of the refrigerator. "Fathers and Sons" was on the kitchen table. Most of the time he read history. He kept Gibbon and Prescott on the lamp stand next to his resting chair. But this time, thinking about Russia for some reason in a kindly way, he was reading Turgenev.

You were probably pretty busy, he said. Where are the kids? With the father? He looked at me hopefully.

No hope, Pa.

By the way, you know, this fellow Turgenev? He wasn't a showoff. He wrote a certain book, and he became famous right away. One day he went to Paris, and in the evening he went to the opera. He stepped into his box, and just as he was sitting down the people began to applaud. The whole opera house was clapping. He was known. Everybody knew his book. He said, I see Russia is known in France.

You're a lucky girl that these books are in the living room, more on the table than on the shelf.

Yes.

Excuse me, also about Turgenev, I don't believe he was

an anti-Semite. Of course, most of them were, even if they had brains. I don't think Gorky was, Gogol probably. Tolstoy, no, Tolstoy had an opinion about the Mexican-American War. Did you know? Of course, most were anti-Semites. Dostoyevsky. It was natural, it seems. Ach, why is it we read them with such interest and they don't return the favor?

That's what women writers say about men writers.

Please don't start in. I'm in the middle of telling you some things you don't know. Well, I suppose you do know a number of Gentiles, you're more in the American world. I know very few. Still, I was telling you—Jews were not allowed to travel in Russia. I told you that. But a Jewish girl if she was a prostitute could go anywhere throughout all Russia. Also a Jew if he was a merchant first class. Even people with big stores were only second class. Who else? A soldier who had a medal, I think St. George. Do you know nobody could arrest him? Even if he was a Jew. If he killed someone a policeman could not arrest him. He wore a certain hat. Why am I telling you all this?

Well, it is interesting.

Yes, but I'm supposed to tell you a few things, give advice, a few last words. Of course, the fact is I am obliged because you are always getting yourself mixed up in politics. Because your mother and I were such radical kids—socialists—in constant trouble with the police—it was 1904, 5. You have the idea it's O.K. for you and it is not O.K. in this country, which is a democracy. And you're running in the street like a fool. Your cousin saw you a few years ago in school, suspended. Sitting with other children in the auditorium, not allowed to go to class. You thought Mama and I didn't know.

Pa, that was thirty-five years ago, in high school. Anyway, what *about* Mama? You mentioned the Arzemich family. She was a dentist, wasn't she?

Right, a very capable woman.

Well, Mama probably felt bad about not getting to school and, you know, becoming something, having a profession like Mrs. What's-Her-Name. I mean, she did run the whole house and family and the office and people coming to live with us, but she was sad about that, surely.

He was quiet. Then he said, You're right. It was a shame, everything went into me, so I should go to school, I should graduate, I should be the doctor, I should have the profession. Poor woman, she was extremely smart. At least as smart as me. In Russia, in the movement, you know, when we were youngsters, she was considered the more valuable person. Very steady, honest. Made first-class contact with the workers, a real organizer. I could be only an intellectual. But maybe if life didn't pass so quick, speedy, like a winter day—short. You know, also, she was very musical, she had perfect pitch. A few years ago your sister made similar remarks to me about Mama. Questioning me, like history is my fault. Your brother only looked at me the way he does—not with complete approval.

Then one day my father surprised me. He said he wanted to talk a little, but not too much, about love or sex or whatever it's called—its troubling persistence. He said that might happen to me, too, eventually. It should not be such a surprise. Then, a little accusingly, After all, I have been a man alone for many years. Did you ever think about that? Maybe I suffered. Did it even enter your mind? You're a grownup woman, after all.

But Pa, I wouldn't ever have thought of bringing up anything like that—you and Mama were so damn puritanical. I never heard you say the word "sex" till this day—either of you.

We were serious Socialists, he said. So? He looked at me, raising one nice thick eyebrow. You don't understand politics too well, do you?

Actually, I had thought of it now and then, his sexual aloneness. I was a grownup woman. But I turned it into a tactful question: Aren't you sometimes lonely, Pa?

I have a nice apartment.

Then he closed his eyes. He rested his talking self. I decided to water the plants. He opened one eye. Take it easy. Don't overwater.

Anyway, he said, only your mother, a person like her, could put up with me. Her patience—you know, I was always losing my temper. But finally with us everything was all right, ALL right, accomplished. Do you understand? Your brother and sister finished college, married. We had a beautiful grandchild. I was working very hard, like a dog. We were only fifty years old then, but, look, we bought the place in the country. Your sister and brother came often.

You yourself were running around with a dozen kids in bathing suits all day. Your mama was planting all kinds of flowers every minute. Trees were growing. Your grandma, your babushka, sat on a good chair on the lawn. In back of her were birch trees. I put in a nice row of spruce. Then one day in the morning she comes to me, my wife. She shows me a spot over her left breast. I know right away. I don't touch it. I see it. In my mind I turn it this way and that. But I know in that minute, in one minute, everything is finished, finished—happiness, pleasure, finished, years ahead black.

No. That minute had been told to me a couple of years ago, maybe twice in ten years. Each time it nearly stopped my heart. No.

He recovered from the telling. Now, listen, this means, of course, that you should take care of yourself. I don't mean eat vegetables. I mean go to the doctor on time. Nowadays a woman as sick as your mama could live many years. Your sister, for example, after terrible operations—heart bypass, colon cancer—more she probably hides from me. She is running around to theater, concerts, probably supports Lincoln Center. Ballet, chamber, symphony—three, four times a week. But you must pay attention. One good thing, don't laugh, is bananas. Really. Potassium. I myself eat one every day.

But, seriously, I'm running out of advice. It's too late to beg you to finish school, get a couple of degrees, a decent profession, be a little more strict with the children. They should be prepared for the future. Maybe they won't be as lucky as you. Well, no more advice. I restrain myself.

Now I'm changing the whole subject. I will ask you a favor. You have many friends—teachers, writers, intelligent people. Jews, non-Jews. These days I think often, especially after telling you the story a couple of months ago, about my brother Grisha. I want to know what happened to him.

I guess we know he was deported around 1922, right?

Yes, yes, but why did they go after him? The last ten years before that, he calmed down quite a bit, had a nice job, I think. But that's what they did—did you know? Even after the Palmer raids—that was maybe 1919—they kept deporting people. They picked them up at home, at the Russian Artists' Club, at meetings. Of course, you weren't even around yet, maybe just born. They thought that these kids had in mind a big revolution—like in Russia. Some joke. Ignorance. Grisha and his friends didn't like Lenin from the beginning. More Bakunin. Emma Goldman, her boyfriend, I forgot his name.

Berkman.

Right. They were shipped, I believe, to Vladivostok. There must be a file somewhere. Archives salted away. Why did they go after him? Maybe they were mostly Jews. Anti-Semitism in the American blood from Europe—a little thinner, I suppose. But why didn't we talk? All the years not talking. Me seeing sick people day and night. Strangers. And not talking to my brother till all of a sudden he's on a ship. Gone.

Go home now. I don't have much more to tell you. Anyway, it's late. I have to prepare now all of my courage, not for sleep, for waking in the early morning, maybe 3 or 4 A.M. I have to be ready for them, my morning visitors—your babushka, your mama, most of all, to tell the truth, it's for your aunt, my sister, the youngest. She said to me, that day in the hospital, Don't leave me here, take me home to die. And I didn't. And her face looked at me that day and many, many mornings looks at me still.

I stood near the door holding my coat. A space at last for me to say something. My mouth open.

Enough, already, he said. I had the job to tell you how to take care of yourself, what to expect. About the heart—you know it was not a metaphor. But in the end a great thing, a really interesting thing, would be to find out what happened to our Grisha. You're smart. You can do it. Also, you'll see, you'll be lucky in this life to have something you must do to take your mind off all the things you didn't do.

Then he said, I suppose that is something like a joke. But, my dear girl, very serious.

ON OCCASION

—

I forget the names of my friends
and the names of the flowers in
my garden   my friends remind me
Grace   it's us   the flowers just
stand there stunned by the mid–
summer day

A long time ago my mother said
darling   there are also wild flowers
but look   these I planted

my flowers are   pink and rose and
orange   they're sturdy   they make
new petals every day to fill in
their fat round faces

suddenly before thought I
called out ZINNIA   zinnia
zinnia   along came a sunny
    summer breeze   they swayed and
    lightly bowed   so I said   Mother

WALKING IN THE WOODS

That's when I saw the old maple
a couple of its thick arms cracked
one arm reclining half rotted
into earth   black with the delicious
hospitality of rot to the
littlest creatures

the tree not really dying   living
less widely   green head high
above the other leaf-crowded
trees   a terrible stretch to sun
just to stay alive   but if you've
liked life   you do it

ROBERT NICHOLS

THE MIRROR OF NARCISSUS

—

Under the spell of beauty. As we say, the beloved object bewitches us. Which one of us has not been in love sometime? The power, the authority of beauty. Her face and form, the way the hair falls like water over the neck, those blue eyes . . .

But in this case the beloved object is myself. This is the spell of Narcissus cast upon me. I am enchanted.

What is the cause, the agency of this? We say that Narcissus is enchanted by this reflection. The pool acts as a mirror as I bend down.

But what if the opposite happened? Instead of the reflection as I bend down, the surface opens. It does not reflect but opens up like the shutter of a camera. There is another person standing below looking up at me. This is the enchantment of the other. The circle of sky over my head, blue and framed by a few leaves, has become the blue of his world.

A MEMORY
My wife and I were traveling in Chile. We were in Santiago. We had gone to the movies and had to stand in line for the next showing. A woman from the slums—called *poblaciones*—was sitting on the sidewalk with two small children. She was selling something from a flat box. Mangoes. The children played by the ticket window almost at our feet. I'm not sure

it was mangoes. It may have been bunches of cornflowers she was selling, or straw flowers dipped in blue dye. One of them, the little girl, could barely walk, a toddler. The woman watched distractedly, at the same time narcotized. She seemed barely concerned with the children, or with selling the flowers either. As you know, this scene is repeated with variations for anyone who has traveled in these countries.

I didn't realize at the time that this was merely an example of what was then a prevailing economic condition. "Underemployment." I first came across the word in a Santiago newspaper. Unemployment, underemployment. As the black market is a hidden economy—it's there but not officially recognized—the world of underemployment is a hidden economy. That is, reality is hidden behind a veil.

Presumably we are talking about large quantities of people. The aggregate. At the same time we have to notice that the language, which is the language of economics/statistics deadens, numbs as with Novocaine, precisely *this story* of the individual.

The story of the woman and the children on the sidewalk is deemphasized and one could say it is of no interest. It doesn't tell how she got there, what was happening at home, what was in her mind when the decision was made, etc. For instance, I imagine it was in the barrio of Los Gatos, in a little house next to a machine shop. At the edge of the pasture . . . exceedingly dry at this time of year, a tawny brown color, becoming the foothills of the surrounding mountains. It's hard to tell from the outside whether these barrios are rich or poor. On the street a mangy dog picking over a pile of garbage—a sight one finds everywhere in Santiago. Of course, inside the house it's different. We might imagine a conversation between Maria and her sister. The husband is out, maybe at a bar drinking. We know he's not working. Or he could be at a political meeting. No sense in always looking at the pathetic, that is, the passive side. In any case there's no food in the house. And Maria says:

"I think I'll go down to El Centro. To the cinema."

The sister says nothing; she shrugs. It's a long trip to the Center by bus. Maria's children and some others from the neighborhood are in the yard. She'll take only the two youngest ones.

"I'm going to buy mangoes. These people like them."

"Do you have the money?"

A sharp question from the sister. It touches on everything, the woman's dress, the shelves, the pot of rice and beans on the stove. Her own house, which is down the street, is better.

"I can buy a few in the market when I get off the bus. And the man gives me a box. Carajo, the price of fruit nowadays even mangoes."

Where these women come from, the countryside, this was not a fancy fruit.

"How much are they, a box of mangoes?"

"30 pesos."

"You're taking a big risk. Tomorrow you could go without eating anything. And there's the carfare. You could buy food for tomorrow."

"Hey, if I sell mangoes every day I can put money in the bank. No, but I could stay ahead of the game at least. If I could sell the whole box of mangoes. You can do it in two hours. Sometimes a half hour. But some nights are long; you don't sell them."

No mention is made of the toll this will take on the children. They are already tired and cranky because they have not been fed. There'll be the long bus ride into town, the mother trying to control them squirming on the seat. Their faces are sallow, without color, the clothes dirty and ragged. No attempt—for this trip—to substitute something better. The sallowness of the children will be an advantage. Nor will she worry about herself. Ordinarily a trip to a public place—where one is to be seen . . . there would be a feeling of *shame*, she would wash their faces and dress them better. But this one is past that point long ago.

Maybe the sister has children in the yard, playing around the swing. She goes to the open door to look at them.

"Okay, I'll stay here. Maybe I'll be here when you get back. But don't count on it."

This is merely a notation. We can only sketch this scene in the imagination. *Therefore* it has no authority.

PRIVATE SPELLS / COLLECTIVE DELUSIONS

I would like to say at this point that I am interested in the fact of underemployment in Chile—and not interested. What is happening in the economic condition of men in other countries is not a path that at the moment we want to follow. Or perhaps it is too much of a path; that road has been trodden too many times to tell us anything new.

In the story of Narcissus we think of the youth, or of the young woman bending down—and startling with surprised pleasure at her face. This is happening for the first time. This story is always new. There is something eternally innocent about this. As if she has not seen a reflection in the water before. Of course, there must always be this first time. We think of the young woman bending down. The novelty, the magic of the world caught upside down. She's thirsty. The coolness, deep shade. There is a stillness. A fresh smell of mint. In a circle behind her head, the sky is framed with leaves.

Why is it that, in art, in literature, images are organized around the individual? It is because the individual is *here* . . . listening. It is his or her consciousness that absorbs, takes in the impression; the individual is one who responds and feels, as if the image in a moment of desire *offers itself* to the individual consciousness. So much so that these characters I have been reading about, charged with this light and energy, stay with me when I close my eyes on the book. They are in the darkness with me. The story moves through my dreams.

HAWTHORNE'S PATIENCE
The writer Nathaniel Hawthorne and his two sisters are visiting the city of Florence, Italy, in the year 18—. They are

staying at a small hotel or boarding house called the *Pensione Inglese*. In the dining room is heavy black walnut furniture in a provincial style, linen tablecloths, blue china, each table with a vase of flowers. As its name implies, the hotel caters to Englishmen and the rare American tourist of taste. The dining room is cool and dark, but with a door opening into the garden. At mealtimes acquaintances are made. The dining room is a hive of conversation, a nest of *intimacy* for a few weeks. The two sisters are intrigued by these stories of attachments, of obscure past histories, among the guests. Personalities are discussed, amorous possibilities (for instance that Miss B. of Philadelphia has fallen in love with a young British barrister and cricket player). Historic spots, trips into the countryside that one party or another are about to take. Hawthorne himself sits unresponsive with his eye on the garden door. What is out there?

A month has gone by. Hawthorne every day steals out into the garden from which a tower, *campanile*, can be seen through leaves. The garden has a high wall and is shaded by avocado and ilex trees. Worn statuary green with moss sunk into the shrubbery. The street noises of the town are far away, there are not even any birds.

At the edge of the pool he bends down, waiting for someone to appear, for something to happen.

Miss B. is wrestling with the coachman or with an Italian miller. It is a night rendezvous; she has gone to him after getting his sign. They are in a windmill. Outside is the landscape of Italy. Furiously she resists; her blouse is torn. They are both standing on the mill flour fifteen feet up from the ground as the windmill turns. The burly miller is trying to wrestle her against the wall, onto the floor. But she is resisting. Moral strength can't last forever. She will succumb finally, collapse in his arms, and he will take her standing up. Meanwhile both figures are sweating and groaning—it is extremely hot. Now more articles of her clothing are ripped off. Both figures are covered with flour.

These stories are the fantasies of the female and male guests at the *Pensione Inglese*.

You will notice that in these fantasies the Italians are dream figures, the miller, the coachman—corresponding to erotic desires. Beyond that, nothing of them is known. Whereas the figures of Miss B., the barrister, and others in the party of American and English tourists are well known. In the dreamer, the figures of the lover emanate from sexual desires, as the figures of hunger emanate from the fear of hunger or the fascination with hunger.

The tourists are familiar. In the grammar of storytelling they are authentic. They are real people; we recognize them because we know them—even though the story may be trivial, even repelling. We know these characters/personalities as well as we know our own faces.

It is the others Hawthorne is standing by the pool waiting for. The others who are strangers. But who are they? How will they show themselves? That is why he is so patient.

This is why he slipped out the dining room door, why he has been coming again and again to the pool.

THE DOUBLE BARRIER

In fact the writer, Hawthorne, confronts a double barrier. There is the garden glade with its gravel paths, its unkempt shrubbery—in a *style* of abandonment, a wilderness in the midst of the city. Still, the disturbing voices are close, coming from the dining room of the hotel, a constant hubbub of voices—whose owners he knows—each with a distinctive name. But this is a distraction. He is embarrassed, bored by these love affairs, every turn, every nuance of which he knows. Meanwhile the country—Italy—is eluding him.

He dislikes it that the audience of the play has become the subject of the play. That the readers of his stories have become the subjects of his stories.

The system mystifies itself. The phrase is itself a mystification. We think of veils, covers, trails covered up and obscured. At each turning of the route a false trail, a false sign.

The veil of commodities.

There is no gift—even the gift of modernity—given in innocence. Without its price.

For instance in India when the first British textiles were brought in, in order to discourage/limit local competition, that is, weaving of the local cloth "kahdi," there was a law against handicrafts. A village weaver spinning and weaving kahdi was to have his hand cut off.

The language of the past names the things of the past.

On what was once his "milpa," the field on which the peasant grew his corn, the paddy where he grew rice, now he cuts cane, now he cuts jute, sisal fiber (for manilla rope).

The labor buys back his bread.

And in between crops, in the dead season, he starves or goes to the city. This demystifies the phrase: "the substitution of export-oriented goods for subsistence goods." But it is not the language of the system. Where there is no bowl of rice or corn taken away. Only cash is exchanged for jute and cane sugar.

What is significant about the cane cutter, his sweat, his eyebrows clogged, his skin prickly with the cane fiber—these qualities have been erased long ago.

The language of the past names only the things of the past. But the machine, that is the system, has absorbed history. The machine has its own language, the language of operation. Behind its bright reflecting surface everything else is concealed, it is forgotten. It lies deep down, a sediment at the bottom of the pool.

MARIA AGAIN

One would think that for the writer—even with a minimum of means, of talent—in order to penetrate the pool, to plumb its depths below the surface, all that is necessary is to stretch out one's hand. To shatter what is merely an image, a reflection, could not be an act of violence.

But there remains the problem of authenticity. Am I able to write a story which is not mine?

We are back at the house in Los Gatos. Maria has been getting the children ready. She is saying to her sister (we will call her in this story "Jenny"),

"Jenny, you stay here. Alfredo will be back later—from El Centro." Maybe he was hanging around the park . . . maybe he's working there.

Or she says: "Jenny, did you see the kids' shoes? I gotta put shoes on them when we go down there. They'll be walking on the sidewalk, there's glass. It's not the same as the yard, where you can go barefoot. I'm not going to dress them." (She's referring to the two little ones. The doors and windows are open, the older children are playing outside on the swing.) "Somebody's got to watch them. You stay here. Maybe I'll see you when I get back."

Jenny: "Listen, I was on my feet all day. You come back and I'll be sleeping."

The sister is not helping find the shoes. She is looking at herself in the mirror.

"Do you like this eyeshadow? You don't think it's too much?"

"No, it's a nice color. It goes with the dress." (The sister has made over a dress or has bought a new one at the department store where she works.)

One could almost say the possibilities are endless. As the people are endless. So many subjects, we needn't have chosen Maria. We are speaking of "underemployment," as this condition is called. There is an occupation/an employment which is never employment enough. An endless migration to the city, a community of the sidewalks.

No doubt Maria is thinking somewhat of this world—the world in which she is located—seeing it as she rides the bus into El Centro. Through the windows of the bus . . . the industrial suburbs, lots with weeds and chain link fences, as the riders speed by. All the cities of the world the same—Lagos, Calcutta, Rio. It is the magnet of hunger that is drawing them.

As the bus approaches El Centro the traffic is heavier. On the downtown streets the bus has already slowed down. Passengers are standing. Maria notes the driver has a kind of fringed red curtain above the windshield from which a doll is hanging. He is making change with one hand and driving with the other. She gets out at the final stop. It's the stop for the central market as well. Throngs of people. Friday night, everybody's shopping. Or maybe because it's nice weather. The market is a large building open at the sides. The aisles full of jostling seekers and buyers.

After struggling to get the children to the far end, she buys the mangoes from the man. He knows her. A campanero from the same district, he treats her with politeness. He understands she's going to the cine.

"Senora, I hope you sell them."

Somebody going by pushing a cart of refuse jostles her. Leaving the market she crosses the street. Sometimes men from the barrio come here or to the railroad station nearby. Jobs as porters or in the market carting refuse or cleaning up a stall when the proprietor closes for the night. Or they just hang around. But tonight she has recognized no one.

They are going down the street. Through a bar window she sees her husband. She thinks it's him. He's talking to someone, another man. He's been away someplace. She hasn't seen him for a while. Maybe she has something to tell him. But through the window the place, with the crowd of men at the bar, the noisy music, seems hostile. She doesn't want to risk it. Perhaps he's drunk. Or perhaps he would be angry, shamed if he saw her in there with the children. She hasn't told him what she is doing because it would hurt him.

She goes down the street, feeling alienated from him, lonely. Now she is on her way to the movie past the lighted stores. As she crosses a street she tells the little girl:

"Hold onto my skirt. My hands are tied up, I'm holding the box of mangoes."

At the same time—that is, in real time not movie time—the tourists are on their way to the cinema. We have left the hotel and are on our way down the main street, the main boulevard of the city among the passing crowd. This is a wide avenue lined with lighted shops, restaurants, trees. On the sidewalk there are peddlers, blind beggars, soldiers on leave. A man half-hidden in a circle of onlookers is selling a wind-up toy. There are the tourists wearing their masks. Street singers. Jugglers. We are surrounded by the gay images of carnival. To this rendezvous we are moving through a series of languages (the language of underemployment, the language of historical imperialism) down Alameda Street to the movie theater.

Finally we arrive.

There is a long line. People have gone in for the first showing. It is necessary to wait. Slowly, aimlessly people fill in behind us. We are standing at the head of the line.

Meanwhile Maria has taken her stand on the sidewalk. She is also waiting, with the outspread box, with the playing children. We are looking down at her. There is nothing to do but see her—at the bottom of the pool.

That is the pool, the glade of Narcissus. At this moment the reflecting surface, the mirror, is broken.

But can it ever be broken?

ADDRESS TO THE SMALLER ANIMALS

—

I pitch through the dark   a heavy-footed animal
Smaller animals take cover   I'm coming
through the dark rift of the sky and through the pines

All animals smaller than me   I'm coming
Weasel I'm coming   Woodchuck I'm coming
Mole smaller than me   Porcupine smaller than me
                Fieldmouse smaller than me

Snake slide into your hole
Rustle your cold scales over the rock   snake
              listen to me
         on the rock next to you   as you move fast
liquefying and condensing your dark links
Worm do the same thing   you are a slitherer also
Spider do the same thing   feel my sound in the tree next to you
screw up your bridges of spit into you   spider
Chipmunk   someone is coming who is larger than owl
Night-flitting bat someone is on his way
            who is greater than owl

As I walk through the wood heavily
Rabbit bounds off a little way
                    and stops and looks back
Deer bounds off a little way and looks back
                    arching his neck
Partridge looks back
Curious to see me who am no different from
                    Everyman?

Why these animals all have the loveliest eyes!

            While I go stumbling and stumbling through the dark
brothers   under the dark stream of the sky
            between the black dykes of the pines
the sky condenses and rarefies over my head

SONGS AND OTHER SONGS

In the barred wood   the Whitethroat
Sweet sweet sweet pensive whistler   the Whitethroat
in my deep wood
in my barred wood

In the limed wood   the Flycatcher
the breezy whistler   and his sister the Veery   his sister the
      Veery
ee – o – lay   ee – o – lay   streaked liquid whistler
in my limed wood
in my limed pitchy wood

All birds sing songs of purest joy so it seems
the Flycatcher   the Veery   the honeyed Sparrow

      But of my own childrens' cries
which is the sweetest to me now
and which is the most bitter
in my barred wood
in my limed pitchy wood?

READING THE METER

—

I

One day the meter-reading man came from Southern Vermont Public Service. He drives a company pickup truck in all seasons. Goss sees him clumping across the yard, head down, in the direction of the utility pole. Or has a glimpse of his back as he retreats from the scene, having completed the job of meter reading, the orange and blue pickup disappearing around the curve.

These visits would be even less an event if the customer were living in town. The electricity meter would be at the base of the house a foot from the sidewalk. The meter man would routinely check it, and never be seen. As it is, Goss's house is isolated. It is a quarter mile up the road, which runs beside a hay field and through the pine woods. The line was run fifty years ago in Goss's father's time. Now the right-of-way must be kept open at great inconvenience to the company. The brush must be cut down, etc.

It is probably this distance through the woods, and the fact that very often Goss doesn't see him (the man does the job quickly—parking the truck at the end of the drive, leaps out and crosses the yard toward the pole) that makes these visits somewhat mysterious. Of course, reading the meter leaves no trace. There is no way of knowing when he's been here, except when there are tracks in the snow or on rare occasions when there is mud. Maybe Goss goes to the edge of the yard where the high grass has been trodden down, or there is an early morning dew . . . there are footprints leading to the pole. And so these visits have a furtive and secretive quality.

One morning Goss received an electricity bill. Besides the usual sheet of paper giving the bill period—June 15th to July 15th and the rate—there was an additional item.

8 people killed in the village of Jinoteca Nicaragua
Externalities $31.00

followed by the explanation:

This amount is usually deducted from your ongoing credit account and does not normally appear in
billing.

This seemed more than a bookkeeping error. The bill, of course, was made up mechanically in the accounting department and beyond human intelligence. One could not hold the computer responsible. On the other hand, it seemed extremely unlikely that such a message had been programmed into it.

Goss was standing by the window puzzling over the notice, when he saw the meter man crossing the yard in the opposite direction. Goss remembered he had seen him a moment before striding across the yard, already with his book out. He must have made the entry very quickly. Seeing him hurry by, Goss went to the door, intending to question him about the sheet of paper, and actually holding it up and flourishing it as he rushed out. But already the pickup truck was moving down the road.

2

Several months passed. There were no more out-of-the-way bills. This was a relief. On the other hand, things were not totally as they had been before. Toward the end of each month, the bill from the utility company would arrive. It was a powder-blue or a mat-grayish sheet with the titles, etc., printed in deep blue in boldface, with white areas or columns under the kilowatt hours and the rate. A perfectly uniform and unvarying sheet except for the monthly charges typed on it in black ink. There were no charges for "externalities."

Still, there was the possibility that something of the sort could have appeared. The first message had been there, positioned one-third of the way down, starting at the left margin and extending the width of the page into the white columns. The fact that it did not appear in subsequent billings was an indication that the first message had been a mistake, though an alarming one. Goss had paid the bill and decided to wait before making inquiries. If there were no more bills, he could put it down to being simply an error. There was no need to worry about it.

On the other hand, he couldn't help but be curious about the information, particularly the figure of $31 for the eight villagers. If it were only an individual bill—his own—that would put the cost of exterminating the villagers at around $4 a person. The figure seemed low. But if it were an averaged figure and the charge spread out over all the customers—there were approximately a hundred thousand customers in the utility company—it was outrageously high. On the other hand, it was possible, that the casualty figure itself could have been similarly averaged out, so that the eight villagers listed on the sheet represented only the fraction of the total that was his responsibility and covered his own charge—a possibility he hated to think about.

The information on the first bill had been scanty, so that it was possible that future bills would contain information which might clear up some of these points. Also, he was intrigued by the phrase "ongoing credit account." He hadn't realized he had such an ongoing credit, though this was possible, and that it kept balancing itself out in the normal course of things. If it had come to light, it was probably because he had fallen behind in his payment for a month, or his letter had been delayed through being addressed to the wrong zip code. If so, this could have been going on for months or even years. In which case the total amount would be staggering. He probably could have wiped out a whole village.

However, no more bills with messages of this kind came. Goss was pleased with his strategy of waiting, which he felt was justified. If there was a repetition, this would prove that what was purported to have happened was a fact, and he would have to face up to it. If nothing further occurred, it would be a strong indication that it had been simply an event or "anomaly," as Goss liked to call it. It would not be necessary to believe in it.

Several more months passed. Goss was relieved. Then he received his October bill. He ripped it open along with a batch of other mail which he had just gotten, standing by the window overlooking the yard. It contained the information

1-1/2 villager killed. Re-supply $6

along with the identical note as to the deduction from his ongoing credit account.

3

Goss was uncertain what the result was of his showing the meter reader this second bill. Luckily he had seen him (he had already checked the meter) and managed to stop the man in midcourse. The meter man had stared as Goss held it in front of him—or possibly he had taken it in his hand and held it up to the light. Goss could not be sure from his expression whether he understood the position Goss had been put in as regards the "externalities" and whether he sympathized with him. Or whether he was annoyed by being shown the paper. It was not his business. Or he may have been simply indifferent, and had not even read the bill. He handed it back and said only: "Have you called Billing?"—the words delivered while the man was already moving away.

This was to be expected. Goss reflected that in all the years the man had appeared on the property they had rarely spoken. When they did meet it was Goss that proffered the greeting, a hello or remark on the weather—the meter reader responding without a word, merely a nod. Goss remembered only one conversation with him. It had happened accidentally. Goss had contracted to have his woods cut by a logger with a team of horses. The meter man had made reference to them, allowing that he himself had a team of oxen he used for maple sugaring. He gave a brief description of his operation (Goss was surprised to discover it was substantial), concluding, he was already "tapped out," meaning, spouts were driven into the trees, connected by plastic pipe.

It was late March. Snow was on the ground. Goss, who had hung a few buckets on the trees, asked:

"When will it start running? Any day?"

The meter man thought it was already running in some places. He had stopped, he said, by a farm down the road. The farmhouse was at the bottom of a hillside with a sugar bush—which was also "tapped out." There was a sugaring house nearby where the sap was boiled off. After reading the meter he had walked over. No smoke was coming out of it. There was no one around; the door to the shed was shut. He had stood in the spring snow to listen. There was a faint sound inside, a hollow, insistent drumming, which now and then swelled to a steady, musical pouring of liquid into the cistern, a signal that the flow of sap had begun.

This intimacy shared with Goss—and the glimpse of a life beyond the formal boundaries of the company—had been quite uncharacteristic and had not been repeated.

Once a line had been down and he had phoned the number listed in the telephone directory for emergency repairs. He explained that a tree had fallen on the line during a storm. The maintenance crew came right away. It was during the night, with the snow still falling. His wife was away. Goss was waiting in his house in the dark lamenting his bad luck. (The power failure had occurred while he was using his electric typewriter.) Down the road he could hear the sound of their truck as it pulled up by the woods and he could see the glow of headlights through the trees. He had gone down to watch them briefly: in the bitter cold one man holding a rope, breath steaming in the headlights; and another leaning backwards from the top of the pole. Then he had returned to the house and remained in the dark for what seemed an interminable length of time. He had expected them to check in with him, tell him the line was repaired and they would make the connection at the transformer by the highway. He was looking forward to thanking them and offering them a hot drink or a shot of whiskey as a comradely gesture. Goss was sitting in the dark staring at the glimmer of a single candle. Suddenly the lights came on, as if by magic. They had simply completed the job and driven off.

He felt cheated. He himself had come out in the cold,

stood at the edge of the clearing to make a kind of contact with them. Why should they care about him? He was in full light but with a feeling of loneliness. It was as if in a way this was measured by the slow rotation of the electric meter.

Though he had inherited the electrical system, and the billing procedure had been worked out for a period of years, occasionally something went wrong. Goss was not hesitant about calling the utility company's office in the nearby town of Bradford. In fact he enjoyed it. Usually it was about some trivial matter, an error in the bill that could easily be cleared up by one of the clerks. There was a young woman in the office he generally spoke with—her name was Martha. He knew her voice. She was easy to deal with, sympathetic. He looked forward to some discrepancy he had discovered in checking the figures on his home computer. (Goss fancied himself something of a mathematician.) He would call to Martha's attention some obvious error, with glee. Of course these were routine questions. No doubt there were more difficult ones which were outside the guidelines of the lower-level personnel to deal with. He had called Billing not long ago about what he thought was an overcharge. He had hoped to talk to Martha. She had been out to lunch, and he had spoken with another young woman—who before he knew it had referred him to her supervisor. A Miss Johnson. This conversation had been a disaster. Goss was convinced he was in the right.

Goss ended triumphantly: "The amount of my bill

has doubled when my consumption of kilowatts has gone down!" It was explained by the official that this was due to a seasonal adjustment in rates, which had been higher during the winter months. There was the appearance that he was overcharged when actually the charges were normal, even generous. This was because it was a period of cold when there was the maximum use of appliances.

"But I don't space heat with electricity," Goss protested with an edge of superiority to his voice. "My personal consumption in the winter . . . "

"What you consume personally doesn't matter. The utility company goes by the law of averages. Your experience of the winter is not the statistical experience."

Goss was outraged. He resolved never to ask a question of the company again—at least above the level of Martha. He visualized the office of the supervisor—that is, Miss Johnson—as a kind of dark maze or trap in which the perplexed customer was bound to get further lost.

4

One day Goss and his wife were returning from the weekly trip to the supermarket. He disliked this event. The size of the building depressed him. It meant contending with crowds of shoppers, the traffic in the parking lot. As they came up their driveway through the wood around the curve, Goss was looking ahead toward the house and parking area. He thought he might see the service company's truck.

"He's not here again today. The meter reader. If he

were here we'd probably miss him. He's distinguished by his quality of absence."

Goss told his wife the sugaring story, where, with the family gone, the man had stood outside the closed sugar house in the spring snow and listened to the running of the sap.

"You have the feeling that he observes everything, but from a distance. He's not there to communicate—if he's there at all."

"He's not supposed to communicate," Goss's wife told him.

"I would have liked to have discussed it, the externalities, with him at greater length, ask him what he felt about it. But all he did was refer me to Billing. It's obvious you're not going to get to the heart of the mystery there."

"The more you worry the less you solve," his wife suggested.

"Well, it was such a small amount on the two bills—the figures charged for each villager—though even the figures are open to question. Such a modest amount to be billed, and so many potential hassles . . . it was probably sound policy to pay and not ask questions."

"*I'd* have asked questions," Goss's wife told him.

"The bill is for us all."

Goss remembered when he had shown the meter man his second bill. He was not sure then what his reaction had been. He may not have cared. But he may have been startled and even frightened. Was the meter reader trying to avoid him? This was possible given the man's extremely reticent

ROBERT NICHOLS

character. Goss had brought the man in on his personal financial troubles and whatever private agony he might be suffering because of the casualties in *Jinoteca*. That was beyond the bounds of the formal relationship of service personnel and customer, and certainly constituted a breach of taste. The meter reader may have taken Goss's outburst as an infringement of those limits. He may have thought of Goss himself as an anomaly.

Goss doubted this. A simpler explanation for the employee's reaction was irritation. Along the route there were many meters to read. With many new houses built, there probably was a job speed-up. Then too Goss had been one of the earliest hook-ups for the electric company when the customers were mostly farms. Goss's pole was far from the highway through the woods. The line had been knocked down several times in storms, so they lost money. So as far as the utility company was concerned, as a customer Goss was marginal. Possibly they had even told the meter reader not to talk to Goss.

Still, the bills continued to nag him. There had been no more out-of-the-way bills. The monthly blue-grey statements from the electrical company were normal: blank and empty except for the print-out of kilowatt hours and charges. Now the blankness and emptiness was a factor that worried Goss. If the casualties were not listed on the ordinary bill, might they not be there just the same—but latent—on the "ongoing credit account" continuously being balanced and cancelled out? Wasn't it a possibility at least that the blank and unoffending bill was a continuous record of casualties?

Was there some reason for the meter reader's disappearance? It occurred to Goss he may have been let go. With advances in technology it was conceivable that Goss's meter could have been monitored from somewhere else, from the office in Bradford, and billed directly. That would make sense as far as cost efficiency was concerned. So there would be no need for field work and the meter man's function would be superfluous. This was technically possible. He would stop coming; the customer would never be the wiser. Still, there would be some resistance on the part of the customer: the human witness as a guarantee against mechanical failure. And because—as in Goss's case—the customer had become attached to him. So the meter reader would have been retained for purely sentimental reasons.

5

His family had given Goss a pair of binoculars for his birthday. German made. Prismatic lens, with a 7x35 magnification. They were for watching birds. Goss often stood by the window, the top half pulled down, when he heard bird song. Resting his elbows on the wooden sash, he would cruise the nearby woods searching for the wren or song sparrow. To the center there was a more distant view over the fields—tops of elm trees and hills, continuous shifts of color.

Seeing him stationed at the window, his wife asked him how he liked the binoculars.

Goss told her, "Superb. Now I'm able to see things, locate them, and catch them in the lens exactly. Before there was only this mysterious sound—mysterious in the sense I didn't know where it was coming from. Now I can identify what bird is singing and even watch the notes pour out of its throat."

His eldest daughter had been to a restaurant the evening before where they played music. It was called Waterworks. The daughter followed the local bands. The one performing currently was the Rude Girls, who were beginning to make a name for themselves.

"It was packed. We had to stand by the bar. But it was terrific." The daughter said she thought she had seen Miss Johnson.

Goss expressed surprise. "That's the last person I'd expect to be there."

"Why? Or why not? It was advertised both in the paper and on the radio, the date of the concert. There was a picture of the Rude Girls plastered on store windows."

"I suppose anybody could have seen them," Goss acknowledged. "And if they liked that sort of thing . . . "

"She was with a date."

"What kind of date?"

Goss's daughter worked as a waitress. "I've seen him around. He's kind of a smoothy and man-about-town. A heart-breaker, I'd say."

"At a concert?" (Goss had never seen Miss Johnson.) "She must take time out from the office. I wouldn't have thought. . . . Well, I might have guessed she needed entertainment . . . some companion she went out with. Though she has a forbidding personality. Probably the call to music was overwhelming."

"After the concert began again we got a seat. As we squeezed through, we passed them. She had her handkerchief to her eyes. She was crying—had turned her face away from the Rude Girls, from the spotlight. Her mascara was running."

All at once there was a bird trilling in the trees. Goss picked up his binoculars.

"What kind of bird?"

"I can't tell. From the markings I'd say a red poll or a siskin. From the cry it could be a song sparrow. If only it would hold still."

In front of the house the ground fell away. So the binoculars' line of sight was directly into a wall of branches. Goss oriented himself by the distant hill, then swept backward and to the right again. Immediately he was traveling through the woods, a maze of impenetrable leaves, darks and lights, foreground and depths—trying to sight the elusive bird.

Suddenly a shape intervened. The picture blurred as if a wad of cotton were drawn across the lens. Swiveling, Goss tracked it—at the same time bringing his binoculars into focus and following the figure as it moved across the yard. It was the meter reader.

The meter man comes into focus. He is on the way to read the meter on his monthly rounds. Utility pole behind in the grass. The owner will go out into the yard, greet him. The two of them will stand as the meter is read.

As if Goss, the customer of electricity, is pulled into the event, the occasion, by the current itself. And the meter reader, in his mid-afternoon rounds, has been pulled out of the pickup truck, out of his own reveries, into the same force field. The flow toward the meter which began afar off and in mysterious processes . . . the uranium mines, oil refineries, or the tons of hurtling-down white Canadian water power, propelled by the same destiny.

Man in early thirties, square face, somewhat guarded look, compact build. Moves with the arms swinging, neck and weight forward. Straight line shortest distance. Job to be done. Now has been trapped by Goss; he can't escape. Nor for three minutes regain the refuge of the truck. He walks with a limp, an awkward plunging movement, which to Goss seems graceful or mythical. Heavy black lumberjack boots waterproofed with mink oil. Checkered green and blue shirt. Red suspenders. Baseball cap.

His goal the pole out back. Seriously weathered over the decades, may need a replacement. Overhead cables stretching to infinity, lines across the sky, perch of small birds.

Plunging over the grass, covers the space from the company vehicle to utility pole and back. What we'd call "reading the meter" consisting of standing before the instrument with feet planted, focusing of the eyes, noting down the number of kilowatt hours in decimals: tens, hundreds, thousands, corresponding to days, hours and minutes, and jotting them down on the lined notebook which he has flipped out and holds in front of him. Pages identified with numbers and names of customers along the route. This page marked GOSS.

TESTIMONIO
As I Lay Dying

Jinoteca
Nicaragua
9/3/87 thru 10/3/87

Billed to H. Goss

As I lay dying. The pain. That, first of all. The sky beyond the trees. The trees merged with the roofs of houses which were of a blue color. I can describe, also, the earth on which I was lying. The earth was the main thing. It was a dried, stiff mud which was holding me up. It had a grip like a strong man's or like the jaws of an animal, a bullock or a horse. I was gripped by it. But it didn't want to bite me. On the contrary, it loved me. It wanted to help me.

The earth was discolored by a trickle of my blood which threaded into a pool in the dust almost at a level with my eyes. It was just lying there filling. It was as if it didn't come out of me, it had no connection with my life. The pain was in one place and the earth and I were in another. But I kept calling
ANTONIA! ANTONIA!

I expected she would come out the door. But I could also see her running through a thicket beyond the coffee plantation ducking through the dense undergrowth with the kids. The kids all getting lost and falling into hiding places, like *garrobos* and chickens, so the soldiers couldn't find them. That gave me pleasure.

The town was absolutely still. Not even the dead moved. Everything was tranquil.

The pool was powdered with a film of brownish-red dust. This could have been in my own eyes. Because they were bleeding. Or maybe they just wanted to bleed, because they wanted to grieve.

Partly because it reflected the sorrow of my hand— which lay a little further off on the stiff earth, toward home. Its fingers were stretched out as if they were asking for a slice of bread.

I no longer expected anyone to come. The town was cleaned out. But I kept raising my arm, waving it around like it was a flag that would attract rescue, and hollering. My eye also saw this blue sky which was collapsing very fast and filling up my house. Came rushing over me with the sound of gunfire.

Into the pool drop by drop.

THE METER

round molded glass   light along the curve silver or mercury gleam   sticking out 5 inches from the box   glass cylinder transparency perfect rondure   A big eye with its ultramarine

depths   darknesses   Inside:
          THE ACTIVE THING
Transparent glass against neutral gray metal box enamel
tint   the word MILBANK   stamped lower lefthand corner
identifies the manufacturer   Box mounted onto the side of the
house or pole   with the cable penetrating descending entering
leaving   Plastic sheath   also subdued shiny gloss equally gray
the one cable goes off everywhere to distant points beyond eye
focus   the other looping into the house

All quiet subdued neutral inert   Except the active element
          the disc rotating inside
          in an interior black sky
In the immobility of the object   *this*
                              is the only thing that moves
          And behind   darkness

Glass container centered below rhomboid plate
bearing the company name and legend
          SANGAMO
single phase   15 amperes
watt hour meter   240 volts 3-wire
type 1–30–3   model AR5
                    (some small words not decipherable)
     clockface   each identical   0 through 9   but with hands
pointing at different numerals

left	left	right	right
bottom 4	top 7.5	top 6	bottom 6.6

single black hand nailed to center of each circle

    four clocks touching forming an arc or crescent
              to frame the words
              KILOWATT HOURS
At bottom of box little latch   plastic seal

FATHER AND SON ON THE ROAD

—

The man who suddenly sang   in a deep voice
suddenly found himself singing in a deep voice
              in a full   unstopped voice
as they drove down the road   his son beside him
who always said Stop   Daddy don't sing
now said   Sing   Go on singing
and he sang in his new voice
        in his new found profound basso voice
as the son was allowed to steer the car for the first time
the five year old boy   which he found he could do easily
              holding onto the steering wheel with both hands
                         at his father's knee
as his father sang loudly
then graduated to working the accelerator pedal
                   with his feet
and shifting gears going uphill
        which he found he could do easily
        as his father sang deeply and profoundly
in his new voice
songs arias medleys which he had never been able to remember
                or sing right
as the son steered and shifted gears   when necessary
and occasionally made minor repairs on the car

the son jumping out on the road
    to fix the pump the air intake the distributor
          in a small way   while his father was singing
and to make a small clutch adjustment
while his father was singing   while his father was singing
          deeply and meaningfully
ballads chanties snatches of popular operettas
hymns and school anthems
          marches arias cantatas
    dolce et forte
tutte et maximum forte et vivace
in his new voice
while his son went on steering
          and repairing the automobile
gradually mastering the whole thing
It came to the boy naturally
it was simply   normal growth
      open to every American   from birth
while his father went on singing
while his father went on miraculously and miraculously singing

THE DREAM *ON MY FIFTIETH BIRTHDAY*

—

I dreamed I caught an owl   in an old coat
and it was my own heart

Hunter   Hoo   Hooo   Skreek -eek   Skyrider   Black
it dropped out of the dark
under the twigs of trees
into the underbrush at our knees
cut with the tracery of invisible black raspberries

I've caught an owl in the brambles!   Under my dreamcoat
it billows out   out   My arms strain
          To hold down a whole field   of wings
heaving and fluttering trying to break out

Heart   when I wake
you'll never be the same again
I won't be able to keep you inside my ribs

PEASANTS

—

MONTAGE

The river, the range of mountains and the road

The river, the Blue Nile, which starts in the highlands of Ethiopia in the clear sky of the Amhara farming people—whom I have called in this story The Peasants, they grow teff, a grain—now flowing downward across the border over the sands arid and flat at the journey's end

Past Karthoum the new city that has risen   and near it the old city that has decayed Omdurman its streets covered with drifting sand At the edge of it the desert and the refugee camp

The highway parallels the great river the flood of water only intermittently visible in gusts of sand like dust On the near bank a herd of hippopotamus the pink mouths open   On the other side a scattering of mud huts children who only a few minutes ago were standing in the doorways watching the flood of refugees moving past

The sandstorm has closed in again hardly anything visible but the stream of refugees heads down eyes narrowed ankle deep in sand. They have stepped to the side to let a car pass It is a Landrover   in the back seat three men in safari jackets officials of the World Bank

In front the Arab driver   And beside him leaning forward against the windshield   the guide
    Who is blind

IN THE PARISH

Tomoda was so busy instructing his sons how to grow teff (the oldest how to manure the green shoots by lugging goat shit uphill in buckets, the second how to weed all day with his hoe, and even the one with the twisted foot, plunging behind the oxen, his hands quaking as he gripped the plow) that he forgot to notice his neighbor had gone over to coffee. This was pointed out to him by his wife, Belaimesh, who happened to be passing that way. "There isn't even a stalk left over from last year. It's all these rows of green little shrubs with shiny leaves over the whole hillside."

"It takes a long time to grow coffee beans. How will they eat?"

This question was answered. Their neighbors went to market at the bottom of the mountain slope and bought whatever they liked, transporting it on the back of a mule. While Tomoda and his family walked the whole way back on foot, the salt bars, peppers, clay pots, and bags of wool which they had traded for their teff on their heads, the coffee growing neighbor hired other peasants to work for him and even bought a Jeep.

Tomoda was talking with the village headman, who generally knew what was going on. He was told: "They get the money from the Ethiopian Development Corporation.

It's a big building in Addis Ababa with a fountain in front. And they get it from the World Bank. It's a project to improve agriculture."

Tomoda's wife got up before daylight to grind teff, pushing the cracked grains over the floor with a round stone. The children led the goats and the cow out of the house to be milked. Tomoda was served breakfast of injara and daba, pancakes with hot pepper sauce. The animals were herded out to pasture by the younger boys. The men plowed, harvested with the sickle, threshed, and winnowed. Tomoda's wife and daughters did the morning housework. The wool had to be carded, cleaned of burrs, spun into thread to make barnos, cloaks. From cotton were made the women's dresses, *shama*, and *jano*, trousers and the men's *jodpurs*. They broomed the floor and brewed *talla*. At noon, they took a hot lunch out to the men in the field. Sometimes Tomoda came back to the house for lunch and took a nap with his wife. Then returned to the field.

Tomoda's grandsons and the other seven- to ten-year-old boys of the parish spent the day in the high pasture. When they were tired of games the shepherds played flutes or sat with their backs against a stone watching the flight of birds. The sky stretched out forever and grew wider and a deeper blue, as the hills diminished to the west. There was only the tower of the church and the mountains at their backs. Hence the saying: "The Ethiopian peasant has his shoulders in the sky."

Karin, her mouth stained with raspberries, was crossing the field of grain. She and her two sisters-in-law were approaching the stone house in its walled compound. The yard was in the shadow of a huge sycamore. Karin felt a chill as she crossed this, and entered the deeper shadow of the house. Tomoda's mother was lying on Tomoda's bed. Chickens pecked the dirt under it. The old woman lay stiff as a stick, her face gray and her body emaciated. The illness had been caused by a "zar" spirit. It dated from a visit the old lady had made to the neighbor; when she came back she complained of a headache and fatigue. The next day she was in hysterics and suffered from intestinal cramps. At the neighbor's she had encountered a *buda*, who had taken possession of her. Some metal work was being done there. It was well known that the metal trades were mixed up with "zars." According to Tomoda, the spirit had entered her from the mechanic who was repairing the jeep.

How was one to pay back debts? The teff went to market, which they took down the mountainside in bags on their heads to be sold. But it brought less and less. This was for some reason no one could figure out.

TENANT FARMERS

Tomoda and his family were now living in the valley. They were working for a relative named Udda Ab. Tomoda was able to have his own plot where he continued to grow teff. They were able to devote fewer hours to this. Most of the time they had to work on Udda Ab's land.

Tomoda's relative had given up his own teff field and switched his whole operation over to growing melons. The valley soil was light with a volcanic base, ideal for melons. This had been pointed out by some specialist arriving from the capital. Udda Ab had twenty acres. The rainy season was in July. By the end of that month the entire field was a yellow bloom. Space was reserved for a small airstrip. The crop was picked and flown out by airplane.

Tomoda told his sons. "Nothing says we shouldn't work hard for Udda Ab, we'll do our best. After all he's a relative. These are lowland people, they're different from us. Though we're still among Christians."

The Tomodas had been forced to sell their land as the price of grain had fallen, for which Tomoda could not blame himself, only God. Whenever he met his relative he dealt with him with the customary deference which involved the routine ceremonial gestures. Tomoda would bow, touch his hand to the dirt and bring it to his mouth. They would give the string of obligatory compliments. He'd ask, "How's the crop? It looks good. Are you making money? Does your family prosper."

"Yes, thank you, Tomoda."

"I can see you're getting bigger and bigger. Soon you will own the entire valley."

Udda Ab would protest, "No. No."

"Are you getting enough field hands? Now that you're a Big Man, you can hire whom you like." Behind this was a good deal of bitterness, but couched in the traditional

Amhara "wax and gold" formula in which an outer layer of politeness concealed a harsher meaning. The fact was he begrudged his employer, Udda Ab, the time taken from cultivating his own teff.

They no longer had their own compound with three stone houses. They lived in a single one. The roof beams of the original *tukul* had been dismantled and moved here. From the conical thatched roof, strings of soot hung down. Tomoda and his immediate family slept in the center, Tomoda and his wife occupying the bed made of cowhide strips transported from the upland parish. Also they had carried with them the traditional iron stove, *mgogo*, on which was prepared *wat*, and the large grain and water jars. Here under one roof all the labor of women was done. (Karin had acquired a Singer sewing machine.) Around the outer perimeter were the animals.

There were fewer animals. But still there were the cow and the goats to be milked, and led outside before daybreak.

Several weeks before, the children were in the yard making a game of keeping chickens off the piles of grain drying. They had seen the midwife come, a woman with the long arms of a monkey. She had gone into the house where hides were strung closing off Karin. They had recognized voices. The stillness was broken by a sharp wail. Then the fainter crying of a baby.

Now they could watch the baby nursing, the mother bending over to look at it, its lips pressed and sucking at its mother's breast.

The heat oppressed Karin. In the highlands, the air had been thinner and cooler. She had married at thirteen. Now she was sixteen. She missed her own house. The young man had worked long enough for his father to put together his *rig*, the large mud-lined wicker container for grain, and had earned enough money for an ox and to buy the bridal presents: the head scarf, Karin's mirror, the silver arm and leg bracelets. An umbrella. She had marveled at this gift which had cost him a month's work.

Cradling the baby, she grieved when she remembered leaving home. She had said goodbye to the great tree. In her mind's eye, she saw the *tukul* dismantled and loaded with the rest of the family belongings onto the bullock carts. Belaimesh and the men riding out on the backs of donkeys, the younger members of the family walking beside them in a line, each one sheltered from the sun under their umbrella.

The Tomoda kin were eating supper. The meal was taken in silence, the smacking of lips and the noise of vigorous chewing being a sign of devout thankfulness. The meal had been preceded by the blessing and ritual washing of feet. They had a guest, another highlander. The lesser family members and smaller children stood about Tomoda. As a sign of favor, he stuck a wad of *gursha*, a chewed mouthful, in Ayo's mouth. "Come on, boy. Eat up." He urged a second cup of beer, in its woven straw cone on the guest. And affected disapproval when the latter refused, Tomoda saying, "Why not? Your mother's breasts are two."

Tomoda was in a good mood. He told them, "We're

doing well here working for Udda Ab, the Lord be praised. Or course we've lost our fields, we no longer own property. We're not as prosperous as before, but we're comfortable. Of course, it all depends on the state of Ab's crop, whether the rains come. They're not plagues or locusts. We have the indignity of being paid wages. On the other hand, he lets us have our own plot for vegetables and to grow teff. So what we want we can buy."

"Tomorrow is another day," Belaimesh said. "It belongs to God."

Karin's baby could stand though she was wobbly. Amete-Maryam would sometimes make a tottering rush after the older children as they dashed scattering hens. Then she would fall down into the dirt. Karin picked her up, dusted her off and put her to her breast. The lips smacked around the nipple.

The children had been warned against associating with lowlanders and not to speak to strangers. "They're all Christians," Belaimesh told them. "But the Devil has afflicted some of them with the evil eye. At night they ride on the backs of hyenas and eat flesh."

The market took place on a wide plain. Clouds of dust rose. There were highlanders in their black wool barnos or in sheepskins, some carrying a baby strapped to their backs. As they bargained they fingered the edge of their shawls, covering and uncovering their faces and pointing at an article with their lips. There was a man in a pith helmet on a bicycle. The Tomoda women negotiated through the crowds. There was the din of hawkers. Everywhere they looked there were pots and pans, knives, brightly patterned bolts of cloth. They pushed between groups of buyers standing aside for a truck laden with chicken baskets edging its way through the crowd gingerly.

At the far edge, they came out at the grain dealer's stand and more trucks. The Arab dealer was chewing *khat*. The sacks made a wall in front of him. A young man, a leper, with stubs of fingers, was playing a one-stringed fiddle, looking down at his feet sorrowfully.

Belaimesh was worried about the evil eye and *budas*. She didn't like the way the grain dealer was staring at them.

The native reed baskets were open. They contained teff and millet. And some barley. There were much larger sacks made of burlap, neatly sewn up the sides with the inscription, U.S. Department of Agriculture. This contained wheat, which the dealer explained was of better quality and cheaper.

Belaimesh asked him how it was possible.

"It's from a country on the other side of the ocean. From a place called Dakota," the grain dealer explained. He patted one of the sacks as if it were a woman.

"But the price?" Belaimesh asked him with her mouth open. "It's too low."

"It's done out of kindness. They don't want the Africans to go hungry."

—

In Tomoda's dream they had arrived at a village near the border. The river descended from the mountains into a pool in which a number of old men were bathing. There were more than a dozen old men. The Tomoda family were at a camp nearby and had come for water. Strewn over the rocks were piles of clothes. The old men were floating in the pool, splashing each other and shouting raucously. Tomoda was standing directly above the pool which reflected an ancient jujube tree.

But when the bathers came out they fell silent. Tomoda watched them on their knees groping over the rock for their clothes. They were blind men. This was a disease, Tomoda had been told, that had afflicted many when there was a river nearby. They were impressively tall and dignified, black, and the single white robe or toga came down to their feet. *

Now they walked off to the village in a line, each one grasping his dula stick. They walked with complete confidence.

Someone said to him, "If you're going to the Sudan, the trail is steep and the river sometimes cuts a mile down. These men are sure-footed. They can lead you up and down over the rocks. They make their living as guides."

"How is it possible?" Tomoda asked.

"They are not farmers and shepherds. Not even metal workers. They are in the guild of guides."

NOMADS

The Tomoda family had been traveling for several days over the high plateau. The bullock cart was packed with household furniture. Behind the cart trailed a cow. Some members of the family rode on the little mules, with packs on either side from which stuck out articles of clothing and pots. Others walked in a line beside them. Each carrying overhead a shining black umbrella.

This was grazing country. Their own mountains were at their backs. Ahead to the west, one could look into the distance to where the sky and earth met in a thin line. From time to time they had seen Afar herdsmen with their flocks of goats and black-faced sheep grazing, drifting slowly over the landscape like clouds.

The light faded and it became dark. Nothing could be seen of the flock or the shepherds. By the campfire shrouded figures of the women as they prepared the meal moved mysteriously. The firelight fell on the opening of a tent.

The next morning the shepherds' camp appeared closer. They could even see their cooking utensils. There were four women and small children. The women wore heavy black woolen shawls threaded with a scarlet stripe. That must be for the cold nights. Through the opening of the tent, they could see a large bed, chests piled with blankets, and grain and water jars.

The Tomodas were packing up, loading their mules.

"These Afar are comfortable. They have everything they need."

The shepherds and their flocks were already moving out.

"But do they have a home?" Tomoda asked. "All they do is follow the grass. What a life! Nomads."

THE PEANUT PLANTATION

They were working for a peanut farmer. The hillside for miles was covered with bushy vines which, after they had flowered, dug stems into the ground and then put forth shoots. Many of the other farm laborers were Gallas. They were from the south of Ethiopia and had heard that there was work harvesting peanuts. When they had first encountered Gallas, their uncle had warned Ayo and Gebre-Jesu, "Watch out for them stealing." Malke had warned them, "Muslin old men seduce boys."

The Tomodas had a few bob-tailed sheep left. These were put out to pasture. On the same field were the Galla shepherds. The Amharas watched them play *go'os*, a game of keeping a ball in the air only by bouncing it with the foot. The Gallas were somewhat shorter and fleshier, they had round stomachs from which hung down a plaid skirt or *kouta*. Some were not ashamed to go naked, showing their dingus. The foreskin had been clipped giving it a bluish tinge.

Behind the living area the workers' families were encouraged to grow food. Belaimesh watched over her vegetable plot like a hawk. The smallest children were set to guard it when the seeds of ochra, beets and fava beans had been planted, agitating the strings hung over the garden tied with tin cans. This was to keep off the birds. And when the plants were up with their tender shoots, there were patrols to scare away the predatory baboons. They also grew a good deal of cabbage or *gana*.

Tomoda's mother had died. The health of Belaimesh, his wife, was weakening.

The Tomoda men worked in the field from daybreak till late afternoon. Tomoda was still served his breakfast and when he came back his wife ritually washed his feet. The field laborers were given a noon break. But for the Tomoda men there was no longer the welcome sight of Karin and Malke, and sometimes Belaimesh, arriving on the field with a hot lunch, appearing through the green of the corn with baskets containing *injara* wrapped in a napkin and clay pots on their heads of hot chili sauce, *dabo*. Instead, Belaimesh packed Tomoda a sandwich and a piece of fruit in a lunch box.

Tomoda himself was beginning to feel old. Returning at night, Tomoda would complain to Belaimesh that he had been downgraded. Belaimesh, too, felt she had come down in the world. When she met another older Amhara woman, the two of them would go through the conventional greeting, first bowing and each touching her lips with dirt to show respect, bobbing their heads up and down.

"How are you? Are you well?"

"Yes, I am well. Are you well?"

"Yes. Very well. And doing fine. And the family, your zana is doing fine?"

"The whole family is very well off. We are all very well off. Our prosperity is increasing, thanks be to God."

"And do you eat well?"

"Wonderfully well. The garden brings forth all manner of good things." etc. etc. The string of platitudes could go on for minutes at a time. What Belaimesh could have said: No, we are not well, not doing fine. We no longer have the land which we owned. When we became tenant farmers, we grew teff but for somebody else. Now my husband and my sons are picking peanuts with Gallas. Our fellow workers are not even Christians. We have a tiny vegetable garden behind a rented house.

Malke, Destra, and Karin were now matrons. Karin's oldest daughter, Amete-Maryam, had grown up and married, also at thirteen.

The three Amhara women were watching the Galla women in their compound. There was a larger, thicker-thatched, roofed house for the men. The women's compounds were marked off from each other only by a few sticks, no barrier to the dogs and chickens. Two of the wives were cooking. The women each cooked the evening meal in turn and brought it when summoned by the husband.

The man was yelling for his dinner now.

"That man has everything to his liking," observed Karin. "Food and someone in bed."

"Love and soup have to be taken hot," Malke said.

The third wife was milking a goat with big teats.

"The youngest is the prettiest. And the plumpest."

Karin tried to imagine being made love to by such an ugly old man. She had been scared to death on her own wedding night. She had fought Chege off almost till dawn, twisting his neck and even biting him, (this was the Amhara custom, to resist as long as possible), but had finally succumbed. At daybreak, Chege had strung up the bloody rag to show to whatever wedding guests were still awake and sober.

"That old ram must have a pair of balls. A different wife each night!" Malke poked Amete-Maryam with her elbow. "Can you imagine Chege taking on the three of us?"

"Gallas. That's the way they are."

On the pasture, roaming with the Galla shepherds, Ayo and Gebre-Jesu saw a maribou stork rising above the peanut fields. It sailed away in a straight line with white wings.

"It's headed for the Sudan, or for Egypt," Gebre-Jesu said.

Chickens and goats, mangy dogs kept running through the compound's brushwood fence. More Galla pickers arrived.

Tomoda said, "There are too many of them."

▬

The river was like a roadway on a map. But the map kept straying away at the edges. Trails led off to the sides, other tracks worn by feet, which—if one didn't have a guide—led nowhere. One could lose whole days.

There had been parts of the journey beside the river, stretches where the road had been easily traversed by the bullock cart loaded with all the Tomodas' household goods and by the burdened mules, with even enough room at the side for the line of the Tomoda zana to walk beside them, each carrying their black umbrella. Then the river would rush and begin to throw up spray, then plunge hidden into a canyon. And the track would ascend. For the last several hours they had been

climbing almost straight up in the direction of the high plateau. They were in the shadow of the ridge. Directly overhead
there was a fringe of grass against the blue sky. On the other
side would be Afars, like those they had passed earlier. In their
minds' eye they saw the landscape suddenly spread out, with
its lazily moving flocks, the shepherds leaning on their crooks,
the Afar women in front of the tent. But as in a picture, in a
dream. And they could see themselves climbing.

Tomoda felt dizzy. Far below, the river was a white
thread, its thin sound eerily detached from it. Tomoda was
looking down directly at some hawks circling. His breath
was coming short and he found himself unsure of his own
feet. He was having trouble with the rocks, his dula stick kept
getting in the way. The stony terrain had become so rough
that he had to pull himself up on his knees and hands.

Tomoda kept his eyes focused on the sandals of the man
in front of him. He could feel his presence. His back to him,
Tomoda could see only the black ankles and feet moving
under the robe. Somehow he managed to be walking easily,
the long white robe falling almost straight, his stick tapping
confidently from side to side.

He was following the blind guide.

THE NGONG FOOTHILLS

They were at the border country next to the Sudan. These
were the Ngong foothills colored brown and marked by an
occasional spiky thorn tree. Beyond were the endless flat plains
of savannah grass like a sea extending from a shore, also dotted

with thorn trees. Threading their way between the hills were occasional "sand rivers" with their rocky walls and flat stable beds, which in the rainy season actually became rivers.

Looking up one of these sand rivers, one sometimes saw herds of cattle and camels and the Boran young men who were tending them.

The Boran were very tall and absolutely black. With shaven heads and with raised welts where they were tattooed on the arms and forehead in the shape of diamonds.

Karin's Amete-Maryam had had her first child.

Close by the Boran settlements were enclosures for cattle formed by thick thornbrush. The Boran didn't drink milk. They would come down, enter the corral and, kneeling, drive a little tube into the cow's neck and draw blood.

Tomoda could no longer work. The work was too hard for him. Sometimes he went to the pick-up point with his sons.

On weekdays, the men were picked up with the immigrants (both Amhara and Galla) on a flatbed truck fitted with benches. They would be taken to a building located behind the slaughterhouse where they would work cleaning hides. There was also a detail of workmen building a road.

With the sun already blazing on their heads and their back sweaty, the Tomodas waited, looking up the road for the cloud of dust that signaled the approach of the truck. Tomoda would remark, referring to the native Boran, "They live well. But they're no longer able to work"—with an edge of condescension in his voice. (Though he was still able to bow, showing respect for the "big men.")

"They can throw spears," Bitaw, Amete-Maryam's husband, said. "In a flash."

When they came home, smelling of chemicals from the tannery, they would tell the others, "The Boran love cattle, fighting, and women, in that order."

"Well, no matter how they do it, they have money."

The immigrants' camp was at the crossroads where there was the store. This was now the site of the migrants' shacks. Karin, Malke, and Amete-Maryam were going for water. The water was taken from a "bore hole" by a pump which went deep in the ground. There was only one bore hole for the entire camp.

The Tomodas with their pots were walking in loose sand. "We should have started earlier," Karin said, "if we want to get to the head of the line." According to Amhara belief, wells were frequented by zar spirits at the noon hour, particularly if they were dirty one could contract a disease, typhus or smallpox.

The line of women stretched over the sand from the crest of the hill down to the bore hole. Most of the women were migrants, but there were some Boran women. They carried washed out five gallon oil cans. The Ethiopians had their traditional clay jugs. At last, the women filled the big *ensera* jugs and lifted them to their heads. Then they helped the children lift their water-filled *gambos*.

The section of the camp where the Tomodas lived looked out across an empty field near the rendering works. One morning this had filled up with a new group of immigrants. They were dark and tattooed like the Boran but much thinner and even taller. These were Dinka from the far south. Soon the new arrivals, the men, were waiting at the crossroads, beside the Ethiopian migrants, for the truck to pick them up for work.

The Dinka built only the flimsiest kinds of shacks. They moved slowly and dispiritedly, as if they had arrived weakened by the long journey up from the south, a place with its own sand hills.

Not long after they had arrived the Tomodas heard ululating in the field. A ring of the Dinka women were gathered around a hole where a child was being buried.

COTTON

Here the landscape was dry plain, stretches of sand alternating with savannah grass. There was a scattering of thorn trees, mostly in the direction of the Ngong hills. Those hills were far behind them. The cotton plantation lay beyond the boundary of a chain link fence. The fields had been reclaimed from the desert. They were divided by irrigation canals which brought water along ditches from the bore holes.

The young cotton plants were a salty green which the moisture of the earth deepened. Then there was a crop of spiky boles. These burst at the seams ready to be picked, then the field would return to brown. When the cotton was harvested a string of pickers moved slowly down the rows, trailing long bags on the ground behind them, hitched to their waist. Whole families picked, children included. They were recruited by the foreman the night before, going through the camp. In the morning the trucks or buses took them through the gates to various parts of the field. There was no way to guarantee work to everyone as pickers.

The Ethiopian immigrants in the camp were Amhara and Galla. They had traveled for so long and over such distances there were hardly distinguishing features between them. From the eastern border there were tattooed Boran. Most of the workers were native of the Sudan, Shilluks. There were a few Nuer. They were even blacker than the Boran. Their skin had a blue tone. They had filed teeth.

Some effort had been made by the Sudanese officials to provide food for the camp. Some food was given away through a relief agency operating out of Khartoum. The Amhara called these whites, whom they had never seen before and who were even paler than Arabs, "butterflies," from the pale-winged moths that hovered over dunghills.

Tomoda stood with his sons outside the fence. At their backs were the immigrants' barracks. His hands resting on the fence, a crowd of other would-be laborers beside him, Tomoda remarked, "They would not have invited us here if there's no work. Now they're obligated to feed us." Since there was always a chance to be chosen by the foreman, Tomoda wanted to have his large family together. "The more the better. We'll be ready for work. And who knows, maybe the foreman will like us."

There was no shepherding to be done. The Amhara young men and some of the Galla shepherds, the players of *go'os* would roam through the section beyond the warehouse and along the railroad tracks. Or they would explore around the edge of the residential compound where the Sudanese managers and their families lived—also guarded by a fence. Behind both the compound and warehouse there were interesting dumps where surprising articles might be found that could be sold or traded.

Looking across the plain they could see herds of wildebeest and antelope running. Where there were smaller game, there could be lions. Once, breaking through the tall grass up to their eyes, they had surprised a party of Shilluk hunters. Their skin was not scarified but smooth as hard coal. They had wooden plugs in their lips and stretching out their earlobes.

Here both the highway and the tracks ran by a line of stores. Bales of cotton rolled by on freight cars. There were flatcars of logs. Thundering by were truckloads of peanuts and hides. Once the Amhara, standing in front of their line of shacks, were astonished to see a train of a hundred camels, tied to each other tail to muzzle and double-loaded on each side with coffee bags from their own highlands. They loped by, their handlers running to keep up.

The children had grown up. Tomoda remembered—it seemed like years before, another generation—when his wife Belaimesh had first remarked that their neighbor had switched from grain to coffee. No profit in grain.

"There goes our coffee on the camels," Tomoda's son Chege told them. "Next we'll see melons flying."

There was no place here to grow food. The Tomodas, like the other women in the camp, would go out into the savannah and dig groundsel roots which they would bring home, their backs sore and their fingers bruised. This didn't prevent the ritual meeting, with its long string of obligatory remarks, compliments, and well-wishing, somewhat blunted by realism. Malke, lugging her pail of roots, would meet another old Amhara woman with a load of brushwood on her back. She would bow and touch her lips.

"How are you? Are you well?"

"Yes. Very well."

"Your arthritis is better?"

"My arthritis is completely healed. Our whole family is healthy, thanks be to God. And your family?"

"Flourishing. Flourishing. And new ones coming. Now we have another generation, what a treasure!"

"How is your garden growing? Do you have enough food?"

"Nothing can be grown in the garden, unfortunately. But everything is in the store. In the store one can buy anything. God be praised. All that's needed is money."

According to the Amhara saying: "One feasts on the holidays in order to work harder." During their long travels, the Tomodas had kept the religious holidays, but less often as there had been less work and less food. One could say, now they only keep the holidays in the hope there would be food. Even on ordinary days there would be no ritual blessing. The men would return after spending the day at their vigil by the fence, covered with dust, and with a gnawing emptiness in their stomach.

"We'd be better off back home in the parish, even with the low price of teff," someone would say.

"But how would we get there? We've left the hills long ago. Like the river the journey's been all downhill. How could we climb up again. Not the old."

Belaimesh had weakened. Bitaw and his wife Amete-Maryam had quarreled.

On this particular holiday, they were celebrating Saint Elmo's Day. All eyes were on what was being cooked, on the little spurts and explosions of fat as it dripped on the fire.

Kamau had shot a dog.

When he had brought it in, he told Karin it was a wildebeest. Karin had looked at him apprehensively.

"But it's forbidden to kill game."

"All right then, it's a dog." Kamau stared at his feet.

"A dog. That's even worse."

"There's no regulation against shooting dogs. And besides, it could have been run over by a truck. Anyway, the Shilluk don't care about one less dog."

Tomoda was in a good mood. Saint Elmo's was also the patron saint's day of his parish. Grinning, he said, "We have this dog—which we can call a wildebeest. Delicious." Tomoda smacked his lips. "Even the root tastes better. It's because Belaimesh has flavored them with onions." He was sitting not on his cowhide bed which had been sold long ago, but on a metal box. He rolled around his tongue and poking his finger inside his mouth, he extracted a *gursha*. He gave the rolled-up ball of food to a grandson saying, "The Lord be praised."

"It's a long time since we've eaten *injara*," Zawditu's mother observed. "It's a long time since we've grown teff." She pouted out her lips.

Belaimesh, thin and worn, lay against Tomoda's feet without the strength to sit up. She had been going out with the others after weeds and roots. These were cooked into a stew or gruel, which she insisted on first distributing among the children. Everyone urged her to eat, but she hadn't. "You'll have to eat or you won't last."

Amete-Maryam, with a new baby at her breast, heard the sound of a freight train going by.

The night had turned cold. She pulled her shawl tighter. Bitaw was leaning against the wall in shadow. He had been away a week and had just come back. He'd told no one where he had been and no one had asked. Amete-Maryam squatted on the opposite side of the family group. The smoke hid Bitaw's face. She had pulled aside the fold of her *shamma* and was leaning over anxiously watching the baby nurse. The baby pulled fitfully at her breast. She was worried that she did not have enough milk.

The camp filled up with immigrants. The day after Saint Elmo's Day, Afars came. From their faces and from the women's striped shawls, they recognized them as the band of herdsmen they had camped next to on the high plateau. They had no animals.

∎

The landscape was bare gravel and shale alternating with stretches of light powdery sand that blew like dust. Against this their umbrellas thrust straight ahead, marched the line of Tomodas, among all the others. On one side of the highway was the river, the Blue Nile. On the other, low hills. A scattering of mud huts appeared now and then like brown heaps. Nobody was in them except for children, standing in front, their sunken eyes surrounded by clouds of little flies. They stood still, watching without interest the stream of refugees as they moved past. They had seen them before. They were always the same, walking along the Nile road which led past Khartoum, on their way to the feeding station.

It was hard walking in the sand. Now they had nothing. No wagon or bullock. No tent and no furniture. There was nothing to distinguish the Tomodas from the other refugees. The flow of refugees along the track and beside it the river also flowed between its banks. Only intermittently visible. A bird coasting, a herd of hippopotamus, their pink mouths open, feeding on lilies. Swirls of dust closed it off.

Tomoda's ankles were untrustworthy. Bent into the blown sand, he supported himself with one hand on a grandson's head. Another grandson held the old man's arm, lifting over his head an umbrella. The dust storm had closed in again. The Tomodas could barely make anything out. In the darkness of the cloud everything was blotted out except the shrouded figures moving. The lone figure of a individual

145

Shilluk, his body pigmented blue, holding his dula stick in front of him. Impassive and unaware of everything except the forward thrust of bodies.

A few moments later, the gloom was lightened by headlights, a faint glow like an insect feeling its way underwater. Gradually the glow grew brighter as the car inched forward. People were beginning to stand aside. Tomoda lowered his umbrella. There were two cars . . . In front was a Landrover which contained three white men in safari jackets. The next car carried supplies. As they passed, Tomoda and Chege had bowed, touched the ground and brought dirt to their lips in an attitude of respect. However, Tomoda told Chege, "They're on a trip across Africa, the butterflies. Tonight they'll be in the highlands. They're giving away money. Better if it's to the wrong people. We could have grown food. But now it's too late."

Two other Land Rovers followed the first one. Riding in back there were other men in safari jackets, officials of the World Bank. In the front seat was an Arab driver and beside him the guide. He was leaning forward, his dula stick in his lap, a tall black man in a white robe. His hand was on the windshield, peering ahead. But his eyeballs were empty.

———

On the last evening when they had been at the cotton plantation, Bitaw had left the others in the shelter. He had walked down the road through the savannah grass, amazed to see herds of zebra running, and on the other side, wildebeest.

He came to a grog shop, a little bar along the road. There weren't many in there. It was dark in the bar. There was a box full of colored lights like a pool. There was a machine inside that spun around and made music. Bitaw had gone in looking for a woman.

A man told him, "There is the river and there are two cities next to each other. One is Khartoum. If you're looking for work, you should go there. It's a modern city made of glass and steel. The other, the one next to it, is Omdurman, an African city, abandoned, its streets filled with sand. Beyond that is where the famine relief camp is, in the desert. There are people there from all over Africa. There are people waiting, sitting on the sand by the thousands. A feeding station. A truck drives up and you hold out your cup. There's not even a fence. They have enough food there to feed everyone. Even camels."

The Feminist Press at the City University of New York is a nonprofit literary and educational institution dedicated to publishing work by and about women. Our existence is grounded in the knowledge that women's writing has often been absent or underrepresented on bookstore and library shelves and in educational curricula—and that such absences contribute, in turn, to the exclusion of women from the literary canon, from the historical record, and from the public discourse.

The Feminist Press was founded in 1970. In its early decades, the Feminist Press launched the contemporary rediscovery of "lost" American women writers, and went on to diversify its list by publishing significant works by American women writers of color. More recently, the Press's publishing program has focused on international women writers, who remain far less likely to be translated than male writers, and on nonfiction works that explore issues affecting the lives of women around the world.

Founded in an activist spirit, the Feminist Press is currently undertaking initiatives that will bring its books and educational resources to underserved populations, including community colleges, public high schools and middle schools, literacy and ESL programs, and prison education programs. As we move forward into the twenty-first century, we continue to expand our work to respond to women's silences wherever they are found.

For information about events and for a complete catalog of the Press's 250 books, please refer to our web site: www.feministpress.org.